BEYOND THE
HIGH WHITE WALL

BEYOND THE
HIGH WHITE WALL

NANCY PITT

CHARLES SCRIBNER'S SONS
NEW YORK

89-252

Copyright © 1986 Nancy Pitt

Library of Congress Cataloging-in-Publication Data
Pitt, Nancy.   Beyond the high white wall.
Summary: Witnessing the murder of a peasant
outside her small town in the Russian Ukraine in 1903,
thirteen-year-old Libby triggers a wave of hate
against her Jewish family, prompting them
to consider emigrating to America.
[1. Jews—Ukraine—Fiction.   2. Ukraine—Fiction]
I. Title.
PZ7.P685Be   1986   [Fic]   85-40752
ISBN 0-684-18663-2

To Dana, Tracy, and Lindsay,
and to the memory of my aunt,
Belle Rykoff Cole Markus.

Thanks to Steve Orlen
for his long hours of help
in the making of this book.

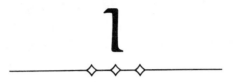

I sometimes wonder whether the gypsies, or whoever they were, worked a charm on the Kagan family as the little troupe walked past the birch grove outside our high white wall that firefly night so heavy with the fragrance of paper-whites. It could explain the many things that happened to us.

It was a stifling night, not uncommon weather for our part of the country. My father has always said it's the combination of the hot nights and the black soil that makes the wheat and sugar beets grow tall and sturdy on the peasant plots and great estates that surround us. We lived on the outskirts of Dmitrovka, a town of 5,000 souls, in Cernigov province in the Ukraine, which is sometimes known as Little Russia. Located in the southwestern section of the country, the Ukraine is the breadbasket of the Russian Empire.

The summer of 1903, when I was 13, was unusually hot. The vegetables came on early. All of Mama's flowers —

1

the peonies, paper-whites, delphinium, and the others in the garden behind the lilac bushes — grew to an unusual size, then faded fast. We must have spent half the summer making lemonade and the other half drinking it. At any hour of the day the members of our household — Papa, Mama, and Grandma Vorontsov, Jake, Rachel and Nessa, little Sarah, obliging Olga, our cook, and weepy Natalka, the maid — could be seen walking with a glass of lemonade in their hands.

It was the heat that woke me. On the other side of the bed my sister Sarah was curled into a ball, while I lay under the blue comforter. I crawled out and stumbled to the window, pulling at the thin cotton of my nightgown stuck to my back. The scented air was thick and still, but it felt good on my face.

From my second story window, by the light of the full moon, I could see Papa's factory, a large wooden building that had once been a barn, just a few yards away. My father had invented a horse-drawn machine that converted sheep shearing into batting, felt, a coarse string, and a very thin writing paper, and the old barn just suited his needs. The wall around our compound glowed, the way white things do in the moonlight. I could make out the shapes of the vegetables in the west garden — the bushy tomatoes and eggplants, the beans just beginning to crawl up their trellises, and the low-lying watermelons, pumpkins, and cucumbers. Beyond the garden, the old stone well that no one used stood out, shiny and wet looking. The tall linden trees that lined the path to the front gate gathered the moonlight to their leaves and sent it

out again across the whole of my world, the buildings and outbuildings, the orchard, the huts and kitchen gardens of the peasants, and the road that went in one direction to town, and the other to Konotop. Then all of those things disappeared. There was only the night looking back at me.

I thought I heard a breeze ruffling the linden, then the birches across the road, but the air was perfectly still. A few dogs barked. Something went thunk — a peach, maybe, falling in the orchard. I heard what sounded like a violin — faint at first, then suddenly wild and thrilling as the whoop of the shofar, the ram's horn they blow in the synagogue on Yom Kippur. The moon came out from behind a cloud, and I could see a long irregular line of shadows straggling on the road beyond the wall. Never had I seen such a strange collection of people. All I could think of was the counting rhyme they teach the children of Dmitrovka:

> There was a cow, there was a rich man
> Walked the cow to market.
> And on the road they met a beggar
> Whose leg was carved from gold.
>
> A cow, a rich man, a beggar.
> How many are there now?
>
> There was a cow, there was a rich man
> Led the cow to market.
> And on the road they met a fine lady
> Whose dress was made of silk.
>
> A cow, a rich man, a beggar, a fine lady.
> How many are there now?

3

I could see silks and velvets and rakishly brimmed feathered hats, and at the front of the line a little boy who played the violin. Two women waltzed, spinning together and apart like a pair of tilting tops. Last of all, a hooded figure pulled an animal cage.

"Sarah, wake up." Her eyes opened, then closed. "Sarah!" She always had to wake up twice.

"Gypsies!" I pulled her across to the window, her bare feet squeaking on the floor. We peered into the night. The wall gleamed. The birch leaves shimmered. There was not a sign of anyone.

"Maybe they'll be back," I said.

We waited a long time, looking at the moon over the birches by the road, over the haystacks, and over the fields. And no one, no gypsies, no rich men from the counting rhyme, not even their shadows walked the quiet road.

"Are you sure you didn't dream it, Libby?"

"I'm sure, Sarah." I gave her a hug. "I think I'm sure . . . don't tell anyone, okay? Let it be our secret."

2

When I woke up the sun was lighting on Sarah's red-headed rag doll, who hung upside down from the top drawer of the bureau. The air was hot as noontime. I maneuvered my body to the edge of the bed so I wouldn't wake my sister. My stomach growled; it sounded loud in the morning quiet.

I got dressed and tiptoed out, down the long, white hall to the stairs, through the back door, and into the garden. No one else was awake.

I had made one of my deals with Olga, the cook. My stomach, which makes a lot of my decisions, was sending me on a hunt for the first corn of the season. The stalks, over the wall from the vegetable garden, were almost as tall as I. Old Grisha, our simpleminded caretaker who did all the planting, had a secret way of starting the corn so that it ripened early. Olga would cook it for me without telling anyone, and I would eat it near the beehives in my favorite corner of the orchard.

As my part of our deals, I saw to it that some of my prettiest blouses went to Olga for her two little girls to grow into. Sometimes my mother would get suspicious and ask about a missing shirtwaist. "I tore it climbing a tree," I'd tell her. It's not hard to get around grown-ups.

Our west garden was about five acres, two inside the wall and three beyond it. The outside acres, planted in corn, seemed to us children like 300 acres. Sarah got lost in it at least twice every summer. As I walked through the side gate, a rickety arrangement of boards that refused to close, I sniffed the morning air. It smelled like buttery boiled corn.

A few steps into the tall scratchy stalks I heard a terrible sound coming from the heart of the cornfield. I stopped and held my breath. There it was again, a man's voice, groaning. I crept toward it.

"No more!" the man cried.

When I got as close as I dared, I squatted and pushed the jointed stalks apart. A thickset man raised an iron rod and let it fly at someone lying on the ground. "Mmm." The man hugged his face with his elbows as if he could hide behind them. Blood and dirt soiled his white peasant smock and his bowl-cut hair. His bare feet splayed from his trousers as if they wanted to run away.

The attacker, his cap pulled over his forehead, his shirt sleeves rolled above hairy arms, spoke, "Going to talk to the baron. Not . . . a good . . . idea." Little rivers of sweat ran down his face, past his thick lips and into his dark, curly beard. He raised the rod again. Wet gray rings had formed under his armpits. It must be hard work, I thought, killing somebody. When it was over he took off his cap and wiped his forehead on his sleeve. Where his left ear should have been there was a lump of skin about the shape and color of an unbaked tea cookie. He leaned down and stared at the peasant, then stamped his foot on the man's stomach to make sure he was dead.

Next, as if he were a painter cleaning up after whitewashing a wall, he tore a husk from a cornstalk, wiped the bloody rod, and placed it carefully next to the body. The weapon seemed to glow with a fierce light, while the dead man lay as dull as a pile of old clothes. The murderer rubbed his cheek with his bulky fist, then turned and left the cornfield.

I don't know why, but I stayed there for a long time while the sun rose over the house. I wasn't afraid anymore, just numb, sitting in the black earth staring between the cornstalks at the white smock. What was it really that I was looking at? First there was a man breathing, making noise, hiding behind his elbows. Now there was just a lump of flesh inside a heap of clothes. If the body was still there, where had the man gone? For three weeks I had watched with the rest of my family while my grandfather grew ill, then slowly thinner and paler. His gentle voice, which had soothed our household for as long as I could remember, weakened, then disappeared. He lay against the pillows in the dark bedroom for two more days with his eyes closed, barely breathing. I was in the room with him when he died, but I didn't notice it. My

7

mother said very quietly, "He's gone now." But how did she know? I ran to Rachel's cradle and buried my face in hers. Mama came running. "Stop. You will stifle the baby." I was five years old. "Where did Grandpa go?" I asked. "He's gone to the new world," she answered. For years I thought she meant my grandfather had gone to America, a land where people started new lives. But I couldn't figure out why he'd left his body behind. My muddleheadedness had become a family joke. If this peasant's spirit had gone to heaven, I wished for a moment that I could see it rise from his body, but all I saw was the shape of him there, some blood, and a few flies beginning to gather at the matted place on his head. I felt very calm as I retraced my steps toward the house. I did not know that morning would turn out to be a window opening for me and my family, a window that couldn't be closed.

Halfway up the stairs to my parents' room I thought I heard someone behind me. No one was there; I started to run anyway. We were never allowed to waken Papa — I prayed he was up.

I turned the doorknob slowly and peeked in. My mother was tying my father's corset. "Papa?" I whispered. "There was a murder in the corn." I breathed out as though I hadn't breathed in days. What a relief to share the weight of that dead body.

My mother looked up from the strings. My father turned his head toward me, smiling. "Why are you so dirty, child? Where have you been playing?"

"Don't interrupt us. Go wash up," said Mama.

"I saw a man kill somebody. He's dead. I couldn't do anything about it." He shook my mother loose from his corset and came toward me.

"A dead man? My God!" He took my face in his hands and stared at me with a look I had never seen before. His eyes didn't leave my face as I told my story. Mama listened from the overstuffed chair, her fingers plucking at the threads of the worn place on the arm.

"Let's go and see." Papa pushed me gently out the door. And as if he were Jake skating behind me on the pond on a winter morning, we sped to the heart of the cornfield.

But I couldn't find the body.

"I *know* it was right here." All I saw were some rocks and a rusty hoe head that must have been left there since last summer.

"Libby," he called from the next row. "Look here." He knelt by a small pond of blood. Only it wasn't so small if you thought it all had come from one man.

"Maybe he didn't die." I wanted to leave. The field was quiet except for the chattering of a magpie. The sun was beginning to bake the earth, lifting from it a warm, damp smell. I expected a half-ghost, moaning about in the corn, ready to lay its hands on us, but as I turned to run it was Papa's hand that grabbed me. I screamed and screamed, until I thought I would not stop.

"It's all right." Papa held me and stroked my back. He smelled of lavender soap. "He must be dead. I'm sure of it."

9

He showed me the trail of blood and the marks on the ground that proved the corpse had been dragged away.

"I'm so sorry, Papa, for interrupting you."

"Libby." He cupped his hand around my neck. "For murders and fires you can interrupt me."

We walked arm-in-arm toward the house. I pressed against his linen nightshirt. So much had happened. It was still morning, still summer, yet it seemed like a year ago that I sneaked out of my room to look for breakfast.

"We *are* going to tell the police, aren't we?"

"My child, you know a Jew in Little Russia doesn't go to the police for anything. If he goes, he gets blamed. He ends up in jail. The Jew has one right only — to be blamed."

"But they'll listen when they hear it's a *murder*. When I tell them I watched it happen."

"They won't do anything but treat us like criminals. I've seen it happen. It's one of the reasons I want us to go away from this place."

"But Dmitrovka is our home."

"I know. You and your mother. My little homebodies." He patted me on the head. "Now, we don't want trouble. We have to keep this to ourselves. It's our secret."

"Can't I tell Jake?"

"You don't keep secrets by telling them."

Of course Mama and Grandma had to know, but our secret stopped there.

Not long after, we heard that the body of Stepan Marchenko, a moujik who worked on Baron Tretyakov's estate, was found in the river. He had been terribly battered,

10

and it was thought he had somehow tumbled over the waterfall by the mill.

Someone was killed, then it was almost as if nothing had happened. Everything snapped back into place just like the cornstalks I'd parted to watch a man die.

3

◇—◇—◇

Lev Davidov was in jail because his bakery burned down.
Every morning at four o'clock plump Lev, his nephew
Mendel Babyhands, and his three helpers went to the
bakery on Chepurkowsky Street just off the market square
to bake bread for the 1,500 Jews of Dmitrovka. For the
sabbath he sold the twisted white challah. On New Year's
he baked lekach (honey cake). And for Purim he made the
dry, sweet hamantashen named after the villain Haman,
who through the wiles of Queen Esther was hanged for
plotting the destruction of the Jews. At Passover, singing
songs of spring, sweat pouring down his round face, he
shoveled the matzos into the oven with a long, wooden
spade. When they were ready, Mendel Babyhands and
the others piled them into baskets and carried them to
people's houses.

The fire wasn't Lev's fault. He didn't start it; no one
knew who did — or why. He, his eight children, his preg-
nant wife, Malka, Mendel Babyhands, and the workers

12

threw hundreds of buckets of water on the flames, but there was no fire department in Dmitrovka and no blaze ever stopped until it was a finished job. Lev was in jail because it was the law in our town that every Jew who had a fire must serve a ten-day sentence. It didn't matter that he wasn't insured and had no motive, or that his livelihood, bread, and the four walls had turned to ashes the peasant children kicked and stirred. What mattered was that he was a Jew, and Jews got that kind of special treatment under the laws of the Tsar.

Mama, Grandma, and my older brother Jake had gone to the Davidovs to see what they could do. Everyone always brought food and help to a family in trouble. Papa was going off to talk to the police. "A Jew in Russia doesn't go to the police for anything" didn't count when it came to helping a friend. I knew that, but I was afraid for him.

"Papa, are you sure you should go?"

"I'll be all right. I won't ask them to take off their caps completely — not to a Jew. But Lev ought to be home with his family — to start a new bakery. I have a feeling I can persuade them."

He winked at me. He has confidence; men listen when he speaks. I love that about my father.

"I'll only be a couple of hours. You're in charge of the house," he said loudly, for the benefit of the little ones and Natalka, and set off swinging his cane the way he always does.

I started off by giving Natalka instructions on how to dust the bookshelves. "Certainly, Mother Libby," she said, a grin on her long, pale face. She was only a year older

13

than I and besides, it wasn't likely that anyone would take housekeeping hints from me. Mama insisted that we take care of our own rooms. Mine, in the front of the house next to Grandma's cosy nook, was strewn with novels, school books, pencils, and petticoats. My three drawers in our tall, flower-stenciled bureau were a jumble of hair ribbons, bloomers, stockings, handkerchiefs, combs, and whatever else needed to be stuffed in them to pass my mother's weekly inspections. Next to the bed, the blue-and-cream wallpaper peeled into little tongues left from three years before when I pretended to be Napoleon marking off the days of my confinement on the Isle of Elba. Sarah and I took turns sweeping the birch floor; our mother's tidiness lectures couldn't be ignored completely. Once, after mother let me know my messy ways were unfair to Sarah, my little sister said to me, "I like the room however you do. And besides, it's fun to help you look for things."

Sarah was different, afraid of loud noises, the dark, Papa's factory, horses, the pond behind our house, just about everything except for small animals. She wasn't part of a pair. No one knew her from the inside out the way Jake knew me and Rachel knew Nessa. When guests came to the house, she hid under the bed so she wouldn't have to meet their eyes and curtsy. She made no demands, and we ignored her shamefully. But Sarah was a special child; there was a secret about her that only Grandma and I knew. She could read. No one taught her; she was only four and not nearly ready for school. When I asked her about it she said she just knew the words. Sometimes when I went to bed early, I would find her tucked in with a book, underlining the words with her finger, taking advantage of the long summer daylight.

I much preferred Sarah to my sisters Nessa and Rachel, two strawberry-blonde dolls of eight and nine, known in the family as the house-children. Even in the summer, instead of swimming or riding horses, they chose to play in the house or to set their dolls up on the shady front porch using a potted fern as a jungly backdrop for their babies. They prepared endless meals of bread crumbs and water and bathed and dressed their offspring with a frequency that would have prompted a real child to run away. When they weren't playing house they cut the rejects from Papa's papermaking into hats, collars, and chain necklaces for the family — and in the summertime, for the chickens. Strangers would laugh at our Polish cresteds waddling about with paper chains hanging from their skinny necks. This offended the house-children greatly; they were serious about everything they did.

Rachel was the oldest and the boss. Vain as the swans that swam in our pond, she loved pretty clothes more than anything in the world. Nessa, on the other hand, was as sweet and boring as the little sugar people Olga made from the leftover piroshki dough. The family favorite, she gave the least trouble.

I finally got tired of playing the lady of the house. No one was paying attention to me anyway. I read for a while and made a few halfhearted attempts at straightening up my room. Papa still wasn't home. It was more than three hours since he'd left. Everything was quiet. The only noise was the scrape of a wet brush against the kitchen floor.

I wondered, should I go to the front gate to wait for him? Risking outraged howls, as it was a rule that unfinished drinks were considered the property of the original owner, I grabbed someone's half-empty glass of lemonade from the kitchen table and wandered down the front walk, shaded by the heart-shaped linden leaves. I sipped the lemonade and waited for a while at the gate. A jowly man rode by, calling to anyone within hearing to come to work in Baron Tretyakov's fields, twenty kopecks a day for adults, ten for children. He tipped his cap and said, "God give you health."

I started down the road toward town, sure at every turn to meet my father. The road curved by the two-story, boxlike wooden house of our neighbors, the Nahornas, who were rich enough to set out pots of sweet william and candytuft by their front door. The thatched huts of the outskirts gave way to the night pasture, used by all the peasants for their horses, then to brick and stone.

The jail/police station was on a side street just before the bridge over the Little-River-Without-a-Name. Made of stone, it had once been the governor's office building. Now dust covered the panes of the one narrow window above the door, and the big brass doorknob needed polishing. I turned it cautiously and stepped inside.

The room was vast and black; it smelled like a sickroom. One small lamp burned in the darkness. The black-and-white floor tiles were littered with dust balls, fruit pits, and mud clods. And if the number of cobwebs was any indication, the place housed more spiders than prisoners, but it was hard to tell because the gloom obscured the cell that stretched across the back of the room. The clink of glasses split the silence. Two men sat at a table in the far right-hand corner; their voices sputtered in and out like the beginning of an afternoon storm. I jumped into a shadow and inched toward the protection of a tall cupboard.

Two men entered the room, their boots clicking on the tile — my father and a tall man in a uniform.

"I'm sorry it was necessary for you to wait so long. In Kishniev, my last post, we had so many officers of the Tsar to assist the populace."

The new chief of the Tsar's police in Dmitrovka carried himself like a soldier on parade. He spoke slowly and formally, lingering over his words as if they were too precious to let go of.

"I understand, of course, Officer Tropinin." My father's voice was stilted, as though he were speaking a foreign language.

"I'm accustomed to a long morning coffee hour with my wife. She is from nearby. Konotop. We are here to be close to her family." He leaned confidingly toward Papa. "He's a rich man, her father. He has a big department store."

The cigarette that dangled from the corner of his mouth seemed to hang from his lower lip only. He pulled off his cap; his thick, blond hair flowed, rather than grew, in waves of amazing regularity.

My father took the seat offered by Officer Tropinin —

17

one of two straight chairs before a desk that sat in the center of the room. As they spoke, their words bounced off the tile floors and granite walls, giving them a hollow sound, as though they had been dropped down a well.

"You were inquiring about Davidov, the Jew we are keeping off the streets for a while. My man who investigated the fire concluded that Davidov was not at fault. But the law is the law. It is not for me to interfere with the Tsar's justice." He took a comb from his desk drawer and stroked his hair. "Besides, you must be aware of how crafty they are. And Dymytro, my 'investigating' officer has a turnip where his brain should be. He's over in the corner right now playing checkers with that man, Klym Sereda, Baron Tretyakov's foreman. You know him? Even though Sereda has probably two vodkas for every one of Dymytro's, I have no doubt my man is losing his boots." The police chief didn't seem to care whether Dymytro, his underling, heard him or not.

"Officer Tropinin," began my father in a firm, respectful tone, "I'm glad I came here. I have found the people of Dmitrovka are being served by a man whose knowledge of human nature ensures the law will be carefully administered." He suggested Dymytro probably failed to mention that Lev, as the principal baker for the Jewish community, paid substantial taxes and tributes to the authorities. "The sooner he gets his bakery open again, the sooner the kopecks will come in. I'm sure a man of your experience. . . ."

"Hmmm, no. That Dymytro — a moujik in a policeman's coat. Well, I'm grateful, Mr. . . . Mr. . . ."

"Kagan."

"That is a Jewish name, is it not? Like the rich Jew, Kagan, in Konotop." The police chief's face reddened; he tapped his desk with a pencil. It seemed that the Konotop Kagan had used "unsavory business practices" in an attempt to put his father-in-law out of business — an incident that even in the telling raised the police chief's blood to the boiling point. "Kagan. I remember him distinctly."

As my father stood up, his cane clattered to the floor. "I have heard of that man, but I do not know him. However, it is true he shares both my religion and my name. And I am proud of both." Papa's back was straight, and it wasn't just the corset. "But, sir, I have come on behalf of Lev Davidov with a contribution from — "

"It is gratefully accepted," interrupted Officer Tropinin, holding out his hand.

My father took a black leather pouch from his pocket and placed it in the outstretched hand.

The police chief's palm weighed the generosity of the donation. "You people seem to have a lot of money to toss around. Just like your 'cousin' in Konotop. My grandfather told me what is inside that Torah of yours. A hunk of solid gold. Come with me." His hand under Papa's elbow, he propelled him toward the cell at the back of the room.

"Officer Tropinin — "

"See. There is your fellow gold-worshiper, the one whose freedom you want to buy with your precious coins. Well, you'll get more for your money than you expected." He twisted the key; the door groaned open. He pushed my father through it.

19

I crept toward the entrance, flattening myself like a shadow against the wall. I had to find Mama.

"Hey, Dymytro, you lose," whooped one of the checker players. As he stood up his face shone in the lamplight. I knew him! He was the man who murdered the moujik in our cornfield. I ran out the door, took a deep breath, and dashed for home.

Sereda was the murderer's name. Klym Sereda. Baron Tretyakov's foreman — foreman for the most important nobleman around. He wasn't just an ordinary moujik, but a man of stature who played checkers in the police station. Why would someone like that commit murder? A peasant would sometimes get drunk and kill — but a man of consequence. I couldn't remember such a thing. Somehow that frightened me more; there was no question about it — I had seen a murder, not just a fight where someone died. The baron's foreman must have known what he was doing.

When I got home, Mama was still at the Davidovs. I went to find her and met Papa walking through the front gate as if nothing had happened. Before I could speak he put his hand over my mouth and pulled me out of view of the house, into the street.

"Tell no one what happened. Understand? And *never* go inside the police station again." He had spotted me as he walked in — I wasn't as much of a shadow as I thought. He said it was bad enough worrying about Lev and himself without having to explain a daughter skulking about in the corner. Fortunately, Officer Tropinin had let him out right away — he was only trying to bully him into bringing more money.

I was so happy he wasn't in jail, happy I no longer had the awful responsibility of telling Mama about it.

He held me close. "I have to see Cousin Avram after dinner. Tropinin wants another pouch. I don't have it." I was glad I couldn't see his face when he said that.

"Wait, Papa." I pulled away. "I saw the murderer! The murderer was in the jail, too."

He smiled at me. "Well, that seems the perfect place for him. Which murderer are you talking about?"

"The one in our cornfield. He's Klym Sereda, Baron Tretyakov's foreman. I saw him."

He scowled and pulled at his mustache. "Are you sure of this?" I was annoyed that he'd ask. "The peasants tell me it's a toss-up which he loves more, his whip or his bottle; he's fast with both. A Jew-hater, too. There's talk that he burned Lev's bakery. Did it on a dare when he was drunk."

"What can we do about him?"

"Libby, Libby. It's common knowledge the baron thinks Sereda's the best foreman he's ever had. We can't accuse a man like that. It's out of the question."

He was angry with me, but I didn't know why. I had discovered the identity of the killer — something that should have brought me praise. Instead my father walked down the front lane ahead of me, his cane, his steps, his back expressing irritation at my news.

That night as I looked out my window past the corner

21

of my father's factory, past our garden, to the dark beyond the wall, I thought about the police chief combing his wavy hair. I thought about the money pouch, and the sound of the iron door slamming shut.

Most of the time I knew just how my father was going to react. I knew that when his pants weren't perfectly creased he would curse Natalka in Yiddish, or when one of us girls brought home a good report from Miss Minna Illichna's school he would nod and say, "Only to be expected," and next morning there would be a violet candy under our pillow. He was kind to us children, encouraging us in our littlest projects and our grandest dreams.

But when he talked to Officer Tropinin, he was someone I didn't know. He was like his business friend, Mr. Polishuk, who always stayed for dinner and said how he'd never in his life "seen such beautiful children," all because he hoped to buy some wool cheap. And he was a stranger twice again that day: once when he scowled at me for solving the riddle of the murderer, and then for refusing to see that Sereda had to be punished. The Abraham Kagan I knew was a man of justice who should try to find a way to turn the killer in. I was sure it could be done. If only I could tell Jake, he would help me figure out how to do it. But I had promised.

"Libby, what are you doing?" Sarah called in a sleepy voice.

"Just looking out the window."

"Is it gypsies again?"

"No. I was just looking, that's all."

4

"Abraham, why do you keep on with this kind of talk when we're so comfortable here?" From her seat near the kitchen door, Mama looked around her dining room with its pale-green wallpaper, the oil painting of a bowl of fruit that Papa had won in a card game before they were married, the mahogany sideboard, the big brass samovar stamped with bearded faces, and the potted aspidistra in the corner. Her face wore what we children called her moo (mother cow) look, tempered with a mild annoyance at Papa that he would consider taking her away from the things she loved. Mama had set ideas about how a house should look, and the dining room was the only one that was done to her satisfaction. He was working on the others — in no way was she ready to leave for America.

Our mother ran her house efficiently — dinner, at six, was perfectly and nutritiously prepared. Old clothes were mended, labeled, and stored in a cedar chest to wait for the next child to grow into them. The world, as well as her family, recognized her extraordinary powers of organization; she was president of both the Ladies Aid Society and the Sewing Circle. With all her cool competence, she looked younger than anyone else's mother. Slender, with bright blue eyes, a straight nose, and strawberry-blonde hair that, when she allowed it, waved to her waist, she gathered compliments to her as naturally as a bee gathered pollen.

She turned her moo-look on her children, but after Rachel and Nessa it faded. Jake, her only son, quick and bright as a just-struck match at everything but schoolwork, had forgotten to comb his hair. Sarah, with her deep silences and a nose too long for her heart-shaped face, seldom pleased her. It was my turn; I studied the gravy marks on my plate.

"Of course the pogroms frighten me. But so do the horror stories about Ellis Island. People being herded like animals or sent back to the old country at the whim of some American doctor. And the boats — leaky tubs. Once a month there's a sinking. I don't want to leave this dining room for. . . . We've never had trouble here."

"Oh? What do you call last week when I had to go like a beggar to your cousin Avram? For money to stay out of jail."

"My dear, that was a new man. He doesn't know how things work here. Avram said so himself."

Mama nodded to Natalka that it was time to start clearing the dishes. None too soon for me — I had someplace to go. I looked out the window — still plenty of light. What is America anyway? Every time we talked about it,

24

it took forever. To Papa who brought it up so often, it meant a safe place for the family. But once, when Mama wasn't there, he said something else: "America is a country for gamblers." America had turned Jake's head; he had the idea that there he could be whatever he wanted. And what he wanted was to own a big cattle ranch. Ever since he read an old magazine with an article on cattle ranching in America, he yearned for a life entirely on the back of a horse.

Grandma Vorontsov joined in. "Bayla, I don't see why you're making such a big thing. We've already emigrated once. We could do it again. Of course *I* was the one who did all the work that time."

The emigration Grandma spoke of took place before I was born. When she and her husband, my grandfather, decided to leave their home, Saray in Lithuania, on the Baltic Sea, they went to the rabbi for advice. He told them: pack all your belongings, hire a balagole (a driver with a wagon), and drive two times chai. Chai in Hebrew means 18 — and also to live. Wherever the thirty-sixth day found them, they should settle. Fortunately, they had the presence of mind to start off toward the fertile Ukraine. My mother, who was 12 at the time, said that according to her calculations they arrived in Dmitrovka, bruised and stiff from the jolting wagon, on the thirty-fifth day. But Grandma, impressed with the solid, well-kept buildings and the busy market square, insisted that the days numbered 36. No one disagreed with her.

"But, Mother, that was different." Mama's voice was aggrieved.

"It was a very big move. And we could do it again. What's an ocean?" Grandma pulled her shawl tight to her back.

"People cross it every day," cried Jake.

"Our dolls like boats." "They like 'em," chimed the house-children.

"See, Bayla," said my father. "Why — "

"Abraham! You are turning my own family against me." Her tea glass clattered to the table as she ran from the room.

Papa ran after. The rest of us stared at the stain as it spread across the white tablecloth. We hated it when Mama and Papa yelled at each other, and America always seemed to do it. I should have helped my mother argue — Dmitrovka *was* right for the Kagans. But I was worried about being late for the meeting at the railroad tracks with our friends, Nikon and Marusya Troyan. We filed out of the dining room, not looking at each other.

Jake caught up with me outside, where the sun was still bright even though it was nearly seven o'clock. The air was damp, hot, the kind of weather that makes my hair spring into a wiry bush. A solovey, the famous nightingale of the Ukraine, sang from the birch grove.

"Why can't you see it?" Jake was still in a stir; his voice, which was changing, rose out of control. "In Russia we live like the horses that turn Papa's machine, hitched up so they can only move in a circle. We're hitched up to all the Tsar's special rules."

I didn't see it that way. Dmitrovka was home. I felt safe there, and happy. When I walked down the street, I

26

would see a Vorontsov or a Kagan cousin, and even though I didn't like them all, especially the flashy Kagans, it's a good feeling to be connected to people. My father's business was good; we weren't rich, but we were well off. Why would anyone want to be set down in a place where they didn't know the language, the rules, or the people? But my brother Jake didn't care about any of that.

Jake was 14, exactly a year to the day older than I. With his narrow blue eyes, broad cheekbones, and aversion to shoes, he was often taken for a peasant boy. Maybe that's why he spent so much time with them, or maybe it was just that he needed to move faster than feet with shoes were meant to go. In any event, he could almost always be found in the town pasture with Nikon and the peasant boys riding the wildest horses. He certainly couldn't be found in school. After his bar mitzvah, the melamed (teacher at the cheder), calling my brother a Philistine influence, made it clear that he was no longer welcome there. Our parents were angry and disappointed, but his irrepressible good nature and considerable mechanical abilities, which he put to use in Papa's factory, eventually brought them around.

We walked by the Orthodox church that towers over the town, each of its golden cupolas topped with a glittering cross, the daily evidence of its power and its earthly representative, Tsar Nicholas the Second. I held my breath until I passed the church grounds. When I was little, my loudmouthed cousin, Hillel Kagan, said that the Russian priests stole Jewish girls, hung crosses around their necks, and made them drink from a special chalice in the church where they stored Jesus' blood. Father Arseny actually treated us quite well, but not breathing the air of the cross was part of my life by now.

The musky makhorka tobacco that grew on the estates in our area had tempted most of the local boys and some of the girls at one time or another. In fact, by the time they were teen-agers, most of the male peasants smoked. So when we reached the curve in the railroad tracks on the east edge of town, it was not surprising that Nikon Troyan and his twin sister, Marusya, were sharing a cigarette. Not that they were peasants. On the contrary, their mother was the daughter of a poor nobleman from Kiev province and their father, a wealthy converted Jew, was the oradnick, or mayor, of Dmitrovka. They were our closest friends. Tall, slender, and dark, they towered over Jake and me. Boys already looked at Marusya. Her blouse was round where her breasts were, and her straight black hair glistened. She walked in a funny, duckfooted way, and when she bent down her legs always opened in a plié. Since she was four, she had been studying ballet with an old ballerina, Madame Leontovitch, who had retired to a dacha outside our town. Nikon was the best looking boy in Dmitrovka — and there was a seriousness about him. The year of the crop failure he helped his father set up a food distribution center for the peasants. He spoke admiringly of the Red Roosters, a group of revolutionary university students who burned noblemen's wheat harvests and painted anti-Tsarist slogans in public places. He cared about other people in a way that was unusual for someone our age.

28

"Why are you late?" called Marusya in her high little-girl's voice.

I told them about the family argument. They exchanged looks, having heard it before.

"Libby's scared of America," said my brother.

Nikon looked sympathetic. "But you learn fast, Lib. And Jake could be a jockey there. They must give out gold cups — like nothing." He snapped his fingers.

"There's no nobles in America, and no peasants." Marusya chewed a fingernail. "Who plants the beets?"

"Dumb," said Nikon.

He and Jake walked on ahead. My brother came up to his shoulder; Jake's hands flew as he talked. Nikon played the wooden flute he'd made from a bushtree stalk, the cow's horn on the end mellowing the tone.

I'm not sure why the train thrilled us so; probably the noise had a lot to do with it. First, the whistle, then the engine and wheels, snorting and clacking, louder and louder, so that you wanted to stay and run away at the same time. And the smoke pouring out of it like breath from a bull's nose on a frosty morning. And the places it went . . . Priluki . . . Konotop . . . Lubny . . . Cernigov . . . Aleksandrija. It went to Kiev on the Dneiper — the old capital, Kiev — and the four hundred miles to Moscow, where the Tsar and Tsarina lived with their four daughters, the little princesses, the luckiest children in the world.

None of us were allowed to play near the trains. The twins' father, the oradnick of Dmitrovka, felt they should set an example, and it was hard on them as there were many things they weren't allowed to do. *Our* parents were afraid we'd get hurt. Did they think we were stupid enough to run in front of a speeding train? That's something I've never understood, but they were adamant. And I suppose with what happened to me that day, I was lucky I didn't break an arm or a leg.

We had found a safe spot, where we couldn't be seen, just past the end of the village. The route to the next town, Grigorvovka, should have been a straight line, but the baron's father had paid the railroad builders to put in a five-mile jog leading to his loading station. This necessitated a wide curve where the train crept along so slowly you could see the embroidery on the engineer's neckerchief. We had a favorite engineer, a tall, white-haired, smiley man who sometimes threw us oranges, even a red ball once, that I gave to Sarah.

I looked down the rows of weathered ties that stretched from town. Jake put his ear to the track and shook his head. With his knife Nikon scratched LIBBY into a wooden tie, then his own name. Marusya raised an eyebrow.

There came the whistle. From far away it always made me sad, as if I'd lost some unremembered thing. The train moved even more slowly than usual, plugging down the track about three miles an hour.

There it was! We turned and ran with it, so close we could have touched it if we dared. "Our" engineer grinned and shouted, and a basket sailed through the window, feathers flying out of it — rust, brown, gold, and green as from the hats of elegant ladies. A teal blue one with green speckles caught my eye, floating almost to the ground. As I bent, reaching for it, my feet left the earth.

I was flying. A passenger, a peasant with a broad, red face, had leaned from the window and caught my skirt with a crowbar, trying to lift me into the car. As in a flying dream, warning voices came to me through cottony walls. At window level I sailed past a family of white-shirted moujiks eating supper at a round table outside their hut. One of them played the balalaika, grinning from ear to ear; a little boy poured kvass from a bottle. As though girls flew by every evening, they never looked at me. Cinders bit my face while my companions ran alongside me, yelling. I didn't have to run — I could fly.

Then my teeth clacked, my backbone hummed, and I hit the ground. The next thing I remember, someone was yelling in my ear.

"She's dead." I could hear Marusya crying.

"I feel a pulse." I watched Nikon through my eyelashes.

They clucked and fussed. A feather had gotten stuck in my blouse, tickling my chin. "I . . . I think I'm okay." I got up slowly; my back and hip hurt, and little cinder burns pricked my face, which flamed anew as I grabbed at my skirt, which had torn all the way down the back. Nikon had picked up a plain brown feather and was examining it with greater care than it deserved.

My head pounded, not from the fall but from the images that turned like the train wheels inside of it. Feathers, the moujiks at the round table, the kvass streaming from the bottle in a wine-colored waterfall. What happened was like a miracle to me, as if I had truly flown. It made me different from the others and I knew I couldn't explain

31

it to them — they would be polite, of course, thinking I was dazed from the fall. What I wanted to tell them was that life is full of wonderful surprises and everything is possible — everything.

So, instead, right there by the side of the road, next to a one-wheeled, upended peasant cart strung with spider webs, I told them about the killing in the cornfield and the murderer, Klym Sereda. My promise to my father was broken, but I was above promises. If everything was possible, I could bring the killer to justice without harming my family. I knew I needed the help of my brother and my friends to do it.

I got it — not right then, but soon enough.

5

"You look like a lion. In your face, I mean." Sarah and I were drinking lemonade and reading in our favorite part of the cherry orchard, near the beehives. She was staring at me over her picture book. "See." Her dirty fingernail jabbed the nose of a lion. She giggled — she knew she was onto something the others would like.

It's funny no one noticed before: my eyes and hair are lion-colored, or somewhere between yellow and brown. My hair is coarse, and when I let it loose it springs out and bristles like a mane around my head, and, like me, a lion looks as if someone has outlined his eyes with a soft pencil. Then there's the flat nose. It must be a measure of beauty in a lion, but in a human female it's something to be "worked with" — or so my mother says.

Our perfect summer afternoon was turning heavy and damp, as if it were hung on a clothesline of wet sheets. Dark clouds were crowding out the sun. Far away, maybe as far as Priluki, thunder rumbled.

"I wish a grown-up was home."

As we walked back to the house, I put my arm around her.

The adults were having tea at the Vorontsovs, our cousins in the banking business, who gave English teas and French fêtes. In their dining room a crystal chandelier lit up like a million suns; the tall blue-and-white Chinese vase in their parlor cost more than a hundred rubles. Jake and I were invited, but we were being punished for coming home late last night. Mama was mad about the torn skirt. With Jake's help, I had lied about it. My brother was in town delivering paper to our father's customers — the banks, the shops around the market square, and the Russian church. Father Arseny or his assistant, Father Ioan, ordered a bale of paper every six weeks; we couldn't figure out what they were doing with it all.

The thunder rumbled from Dmitrovka now. Sarah and I ran through the front door right into Rachel.

"We were coming to find you," said Rachel.

"It's so funny out," said Nessa as she pulled me inside. The light behind us had turned the color of weak tea; while the air held its breath, our horses whinnied.

"Come on, let's play something. Statues."

Soon the three little girls were frozen still, their arms flung out or twisted like the poor cripples who came to town on market day to beg. They were so intent on their game, they didn't notice the shadows that threatened to swallow them or that the room, even the very house, hovered gloomily around their still forms. The thunder clapped in our garden, and as the girls hurled themselves

34

at me, Natalka rushed in and began to sweep a patch of floor over and over, the broom straws scratching at my heels.

As the rain began, dogs barked. When the next bolt crashed it lit up a scene outside the window I could scarcely believe. A tall man with a forest-green velvet jacket and a determined stride led a ragtag collection of people up our front walk. A woman in dark red whirled about, becoming two women. Luminous in the brief light, a red animal cage pulled by a hunchback lurched toward the house. A little girl, her hands in the air, skipped backwards while a boy in a feathered hat trailed behind.

> There was a cow, there was a rich man
> Walked the cow to market.
> And on the road they met a beggar
> Whose leg was carved from gold.

> A cow, a rich man, a beggar.
> How many are there now?

> There was a cow, there was a rich man
> Led the cow to market.
> And on the road they met a fine lady
> Whose dress was silky-red.

> A cow, a rich man, a beggar, a fine lady.
> How many are there now?

I opened the door, and they crowded into our small entry hall, one by one, filling it with the smells of wet cloth and the sounds of a strange language.

"Oh, how wet you are. I'll get some towels." From the linen closet I brought all the towels I could carry. Already the rug was becoming a soggy sponge. And Rachel, Nessa, and Natalka stood still as statues surveying the visitors, while Sarah peeked from behind my skirt.

"Don't just stand there, Natalka. Get some tea for our guests."

There were ten of them, drying themselves carefully — five men, three women, and the two children. They dropped their towels on the carpet; they touched Nessa's coppery curls. Someone tapped my shoulder and when I looked, it could have been any of them. A man with a scar where his right laugh line ought to have been nodded like a bird bending for a drink. They spoke to each other in a language full of *shhh*'s and *ouw*'s. The hunchbacked man, who was about my size, put his face right to mine — his olive skin was young, but his hair was white.

The man in green velvet called out something sharp, and my guests moved back against the walls, against the table that held our silver box. "*Shhh.*" "*Ouw.*" Then they were quiet.

"My dear young lady, St. Sava will bless you." His Russian was excellent. With a flourish of his plumed hat, he bowed, then laid his hand on the hunchback's shoulder. "My brother would ask a favor. His falcon is outside in a cage. Could he bring it in out of the rain? Like us, it is accustomed to a better life than the one of the road."

I nodded.

Nessa stared at the little boy, who shivered as he gripped a violin to his narrow body.

36

How thoughtless I had been. "Come into the kitchen."

As Natalka and Rachel handed out glasses of tea, the strangers huddled around the stove as if it were the sun itself. They warmed their hands on the cloudy glasses and breathed in the fragrant steam. They settled themselves, some at the table, some on the floor, like a flock of the long-legged shore birds that sometimes came to our pond. As a red-velvet woman seated herself her foot, bare and cracked, poked out of her skirt. The little girl sipped her tea, occasionally running her tongue along the rim of the glass. She blushed when I looked at her. Her golden slippers seemed as if they'd never been walked in. The hunchback bounded in, his falcon stowed safely away, and grabbed his tea, blinking his little eyes around the kitchen.

"Let me tell you our story," said the green-velvet man from his place at the table. He adjusted the creases in his worn trousers and drained the scalding tea, then daintily blotted his lips with a large handkerchief of frayed silk. "We are Serbs of an old and noble family. I am Count Dusan of Belgrade-on-the-Danube. My daughter was in the court of the very royal king Obrenovic and his queen, Draga. They were murdered, you know, our king and queen."

Papa had told me about the revolt in Serbia, a little country in the Balkan Mountains, west of Russia. The king and his supporters were killed by a rival dynasty; my father told me because he thought it was important to know what was going on in the world.

The frail boy with the violin pulled Rachel's hair. Both Nessa and Rachel kicked him. For Sarah, the pull of a queen named Draga was strong, and she came out from behind my skirt.

"Since 1815 there has been an Obrenovic king. We can't go back. Our lives are broken things. . . . Might. . . . Do you think we might have something to eat? The children. We asked at Baron Tretyakov's estate, but someone cracked a whip at us. He must have thought we were gypsies. It is a common misconception." The troupe watched his face as if their eyes could do the work of ears and make sense of this strange Russian language.

"Get out the dinner, Natalka."

"I won't do that. Olga made the dinner for you all to eat tonight when they come home."

"Open the oven," I said.

My sisters looked from Natalka to me. The visitors whispered.

Natalka sobbed into her apron. "Your mother will kill me."

"She won't get a chance. I'm going to do it first," I said as I took the dinner from the oven, while Natalka stood in the broom corner, her face buried in a dustrag, her poor shoulders heaving. She didn't understand that these people were royalty, even though they had lost their kingdom, and it was appropriate for a maid to serve them in style. But the house-children, more aware than the servinggirl, scurried to set out the silver Friday-night candlesticks and the fine linen cloth Grandma had brought with her in the balagole from Saray, all in homage to a secondhand acquaintance with Queen Draga.

I helped the little girl — she must have been about six

— to the table. Her dark hair was glossy and she seemed well cared for. But not the others; up close the red-velvet skirts had places where the cloth was rubbed bare, and in one of them a hatpin fastened the edges of a ragged hole. The two women who wore them were dark and haughty with arched eyebrows and flared nostrils. They spoke only to each other. The third woman was younger and plainer, and she said not a word.

Since there was no room for us at the table, we hung back and watched. Sarah stood next to the little girl, mesmerized by the child's golden slippers. Nessa and Rachel stationed themselves at the head of the table by Count Dusan, while I brought a chair from the kitchen and sat at his other side. This was the first dinner party I'd given, and I didn't want to miss a thing. It didn't matter that my guests were poor and starving, or that Natalka, whom Rachel had wheedled from her corner with promises that she would tell Mama, "Libby was so nasty and bossy there was nothing else you could do," never stopped crying as she served the meal. Even the Count's dazzling smile failed to stanch her tears. But the tablecloth was elegant and the candlesticks provided a gleam of affluence that, as Grandma says, only well-polished silver brings to a room.

The pale-green cabbage rolls were perfectly stuffed — I had helped Olga with that. The grains of kasha were separate and fluffy, and it was a miracle that Olga's spicy honey cake had risen to such heights, so full was it of raisins, currants, and walnuts.

"Was Queen Draga beautiful?" asked Rachel.

The Count nodded his head in wonder and his eyes took on a faraway look. "She was dark as the midnight sky and twice as beautiful!"

"What happened to the children?" asked Nessa, a deep frown clouding her sunny face.

"What children, my dear?" As his hands flew up, fluttering in the air like two pigeons waiting to be called home, a gold ring with a red stone flashed with startling brilliance. "Ah, you must mean little royal heirs. There were none. Alas! We could begin a new dynasty."

My party must have presented those people with their first decent meal in weeks, but you wouldn't have known it. They ate as if they were still at King Obrenovic's table, with one difference — they ate everything. Their plates after dinner were as clean as they were when Nessa and Rachel put them on the table. I had Natalka bring out the next day's loaf of bread so they could sop up every last bit.

The room was quiet except for the rain that pattered gently, steadily on the roof, on the front porch, and dripped in irregular splats from the eaves. Count Dusan cupped his chin and dreamed, his ring glowing red as blood; his eyes caught mine, and he slid the gold band onto my finger. It felt warm.

"It was given to me by the sister of our king, many years ago. I did her a favor. She said there was a power in it — I don't know."

"It's beautiful," I said as I handed it back.

The Serbs began to sit on the edges of their chairs — they cocked their heads as if waiting for a call from someone outside in the rain. The scar-faced man whispered to the woman next to him, and she raised an arched eyebrow. The hunchback pulled on the hood of the cloak he had never shed.

I packed up their sacks with all the food I could lay my hands on: zwieback, cherries, pickles, and raisins, finishing off with the entire bin of cubed sugar.

The count beckoned my sisters and, one by one, he laid his hand on their heads and said some words in his own language. The rest of the troupe nodded. "*Sshhh. Ouw.*"

"My dear child . . . someday we will repay you."

I opened the door. The wind was howling and pushing at the rain. The thunder pushed back as the troupe hoisted their sacks and started out. I wanted to invite them to stay, but Mama and the others would be home any minute. We never asked them where they were going, nor did they say. They set off down the gravel path, under the waving trees, never looking back. A bolt of lightning struck a few yards from the old well; I buried my head in my hands and when I opened my eyes they were gone.

I ran down the path with my sisters trailing after. "There," called Sarah pointing to some figures by the gate. But it was my parents and grandmother hurrying toward the house.

"Did you see them?" called Rachel. "The duke and the rest?"

"You must have seen them!" cried Nessa.

"We haven't seen a soul all the way home," said Papa. "Who else would be crazy enough to go out in a storm like this? I'm hungry for my dinner. Anna gave us cucumber sandwiches the size of my thumbnail."

41

My sisters and I ran out the gate. To the east toward Konotop, the Misyuras' one-room hut, fuel straw stacked in front of it, squatted next to the road, while to the west, in the direction of town, the rain beat on the tin roof of the horse-changing shed as the white-trunked birches swayed madly in the wind. There was nothing else to be seen.

Our parents had come home from the Vorontsovs with the news that people around Dmitrovka had been missing things — a bread knife, a favorite horsewhip, a kozukh (a sheep fur coat with the fur worn on the outside), a keg of red Crimean wine. It was odd — everyone always left things out and nothing was ever taken. Grandma accused the Serbs, calling them gypsies, but I defended them and, unexpectedly, my mother and father sided with me. Everything the visitors told us agreed with what had actually happened in Serbia, except that Papa had never heard of Count Dusan of Belgrade-on-the-Danube. But then, as he said, he was no authority on the matter and he and Mama didn't mind eating boiled potatoes instead of the stuffed cabbage Olga had prepared. They said I'd earned a mitzvah (blessing). When I was finally allowed to go to my room, I had a strange feeling, as if I'd escaped from some danger. It must have been that I was relieved at not being punished for giving away our dinner.

6

This was the summer of family performances. Every summer I can remember is stamped by a momentous happening or by the repetition of a series of events that color it. Six years before, the summer I was seven, Aunt Lilia, Grandma's second cousin once removed, came from Saray with her five children for a short visit, broke her ankle in a game of hunt-tag, and ended up staying until September. She had been on the stage and never went anywhere without her morocco leather wig case. Every morning — that is, when she could still walk — she would come downstairs, her hair a different color and style. I loved best the waist-length yellow ringlets that, combined with her ample figure, made her look like the painting of the Rhine-maiden in my teacher Minna Illichna's music room. The five children, ages one to ten, were always underfoot and never helped one bit around the house. Nor did Aunt Lilia, even before she broke her ankle.

My Grandma Vorontsov, a stern, no-nonsense sort of

woman, was putty in the fluttery white hands of Aunt Lilia. Since hardly anyone met Grandma's high standards for character and seriousness of purpose, what she saw in Aunt Lilia was a mystery to everyone. Maybe it was her cousin's plump beauty. Grandma, a large, square woman who appeared to be carved from granite like the statue of General Kutuzov in the town square, was contemptuous of thin, delicate women. "No flesh, no gumption," she'd say. I used to wonder if that's why she and my slender mother, her own daughter, have such a hard time together, but now I think I know another reason.

My being thin has not affected my relationship with my grandmother. We are very close. She talks to me about what is in her heart; she tells me stories of the olden days. "Someone should hear these things," she says. "Maybe when you're older, you'll write them down. I see your compositions — you have the gift."

Three summers before, when Papa was inventing his machine, she took complete charge of the household. Mama had all she could do to keep Papa from tearing out his thick, white hair, which had grayed by the time he was 28 — 10 years before. He has always invented things — a household pea sheller, a cider press that he sold for 25 rubles right after he and my mother were married, and a knitting machine. He would have made a lot of money from the knitting machine, but he couldn't get the lock-stitch right — none of the scarves had an end to them. He tried everything until finally he just took some scissors and cut one right off the machine. Mama wore it, a service-able blue, for a few weeks. After it unraveled one size, she passed it on to me, and so it went down through the family, ending up as a tiny ball of yarn in Mama's wooden-handled knitting bag.

Last summer, after she caught Nessa and Rachel in the closet long past their bedtime, drawing a likeness of our cousin Anna Vorontsov by the light of a kerosene lamp, my mother decided that our family burned with a hidden artistic talent. Easels were set up on the long front porch, brilliant watercolor paints arrived in a brown paper parcel from Konotop, and at least three nights a week we sat in the beautiful summer twilight and painted. My mother did flowers — the ruffled pink peonies were her favorites. All the browns and blacks were at Jake's easel, for the horses. The house-children, whose talent shone brighter in the closet by lamplight than on the front porch in the late-day sun, painted whatever came into their heads — skies, kittens, houses, dolls — but somehow they all looked the same. Sarah, who was only three, "helped" me, and I needed it. I could never get the right mixture of paint and water, so my pictures were either faint or sticky, and my squares of color always had holes in the bottom where the paint had been washed away. The one time I got the old well down with a certain degree of accuracy, Grandma complimented me on my likeness of the barn. While we painted, Grandma knitted — "I'm past the age when I can take up something new" — but I think she didn't want to do it because it was Mama's idea.

When he wasn't busy with his accounts, Papa would pick up the brush, and it turned out that he was the only one of us who was any good. Maybe it was the same gift that allowed him to invent things, but his horses flew across the paper, and his well was instantly recognizable.

My mother thought an afternoon of tea and watercolors would be uplifting for our relatives, so one late August day the front porch teamed with fashionable Vorontsovs and loud, pushy Kagans, drinking tea and lemonade, nibbling on sand cakes, and regarding, with solemn faces, our summer's output, which Jake had hung on a rope that stretched across the porch. Everyone, from jolly Uncle Boris, the wife of my father's sister, Rebecca, to prim six-year-old Katerina Vorontsov, pronounced the art to be splendid. Mama glowed.

But it was my father who decreed this the summer of family performances. "School is out. Minds vegetate. We need to keep them humming." So Papa set up a mind-improvement program. Twice a week, on Tuesdays and Thursdays after dinner, we lined up the front-porch chairs and listened as one (or more) family member "stimulated" the minds of the rest of us. It was my favorite of all our summer projects; Rachel and Nessa, who loved to show off, liked it too. But Jake didn't go for anything that might be related to reading and Sarah was so shy, no one expected her to perform. The rules were loose. We could memorize a passage from the Bible, give a dramatic reading, make up a skit, or discuss a political or philosophical theory. "The mind's a sponge — it sucks it all up." Papa was ready for anything, and he expected the same from us. Woe be to any child or adult — for they had their turn, too — who came unprepared.

Sarah had fallen in love with a picture on a calendar

that Aunt Lilia had sent us — a picture of a little girl on a big, black horse. She wanted to be that girl, so Jake promised he would ride with her and help her get over the fear of horses. Now he was going back on his promise because he wanted to race against some boys who were coming over from Grigorovka. Sarah was hurt, but in front of Jake, whom she adored, she managed a stiff little smile and said it didn't matter. I don't get mad at Jake very often, but I was furious as it was the first time Sarah had made an effort to overcome any of her fears.

I offered to substitute for Jake, but she just shook her head. I ride well enough, but Jake was the family expert on horses and I guess she didn't trust me the way she did him. It had to be made up to her somehow. Maybe if she could learn to do something other people would envy, but what can a four-year-old do? Then I remembered her reading. Tuesday was my night to perform. I was going to recite a poem I had written about friendship; Marusya was the inspiration for it. But I could make Sarah the surprise performer — with my coaching she could give a reading exhibition that would astonish everyone.

I wasn't sure how she would feel about all this, but when I found her padding down the hall in my old white robe she said, "I'll learn to read anything you want. That's something I *know* I can do." Why hadn't I thought to ask her before?

We decided she would read *Daughters of the Lily Pond*, the book Grandma was reading to Rachel and Nessa. The house-children made a game of taking on the personality of every heroine they read about, even dressing up to fit the part. Sarah was charmed by the long skirts and droopy shawls they pinned together with material from our mother's scrap bag, while their soulful looks and bountiful sighs made her giggle.

I was a little worried. Tuesday was only four days away. But Sarah turned out to be a born student—possibly even a reading genius — who mastered *Daughters of the Lily Pond*, a dark-green volume with gilt letters and a picture of two golden-haired girls standing on a giant water-lily pad, as if it were an alphabet book. And our lessons seemed to ease her shyness; when Aunt Rebecca and Uncle Boris came to call she actually stayed in the room and smiled. I've never seen her so happy as during those four days.

Tuesday afternoon it rained, but by evening it had cleared. The sky was blue with a clean, rainy glow and the few puffy clouds were outlined in gray. The air smelled like dark, wet earth, and the ferns on the front porch steps glowed greenly from their white urns.

We gathered our chairs, together, everyone looking expectantly at me. When I announced that Sarah would take my place, no one said a word. As she stepped in front of us and curtsied the way we were taught to do, her eyes, big and dark as the purple-black pansies Mama grew, met mine. She was afraid. So was I.

"The day had finally come. Jeanette and Marianne . . ." She began.

Rachel whispered in Nessa's ear; Nessa ignored her.

"Everywhere on the night air there lingered the breath of roses." Page two was going as smoothly as page one.

Mama was entranced; Grandma let her embroidery drop to her lap.

"The fountain splashed in gay —"

"Sarah, I don't believe it's you." Mama couldn't let her go any farther without rushing up and hugging her. "Why didn't you tell us before you could read like this? A real Vorontsov, isn't she, Mother! Here, read this." She handed Sarah a pamphlet from her sewing basket that my little sister should have been able to decipher easily. But instead, she stood in front of her family, staring at the gray booklet as if it were written in Serbian. One tear made its way down her cheek, then another — she didn't even try to blink them back. As she flattened the pamphlet against her face, I started toward her, but Grandma held me back.

"I can't . . ." She lowered the book. Tear stripes staining her cheeks, her eyes too bright, she looked Mama straight in the eye. "I can't read this one."

Mother accused me of helping Sarah memorize *Daughters of the Lily Pond*. I tried to explain that she could read anything, but the unfamiliar book had frozen her. It was Papa who came to the rescue, pulling her onto his lap, crooning praises at her sad little face, stroking her cheek with a white rose from his lapel. Then everyone joined in: Mother apologized, Rachel and Nessa got in a shoving match patting her on the head, Jake made extravagant promises regarding horses, and Grandma, her eyes tearing, said, "Just like my David." But Sarah wouldn't be comforted — at least not then. She hadn't performed the way she knew she could.

That night I tucked the faded blue comforter around

49

her. "Papa is going to buy me a book tomorrow. He's proud of me," she said, curling up in the big bed.

"I'm proud of you, too." I kissed her good-night. It was late. I crawled into bed beside her and held her hand and would have cried myself if she couldn't have heard me. Several times that night I woke up thinking Sarah called me, but she was sleeping.

I got up early in the morning and went for a walk in the birch grove across the road where I first saw the Serbs or gypsies. Pinned to a tree trunk with a hat pin was a partly burned piece of paper with writing on it — writing as thin as a spider web. Here is what it said:

> Heart hungry, I never crossed
> Your threshold with a grief
> That was not mine.

What an odd poem — if that's what it was — and what happened to the rest of it? I took it home and tossed it into my bureau drawer.

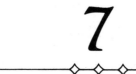

7

He always wished that his daughter had my brains and chutzpah — he told me so almost every time we met. That's why, when Cousin Avram needed a child for the party, he took me. That hot August the Vorontsov children were vacationing with their mother at a hotel on the Black Sea. Avram was invited to the name-day celebration for Baron Tretyakov's twelve-year-old daughter, Tatiana. The invitation read ". . . and children," so he thought he had better bring one.

I wore a white lawn dress with a blue silk sash that my cousin's seamstress made for me. Even the hem of that dress was a work of art, the tiniest white stitches, as perfect as a row of baby teeth. Grandma lent me her locket etched with fleur-de-lys. "A little gold is always good." Mama dabbed some perfume on my earlobes and I smelled of lime blossoms. Natalka fixed my hair the way the peasant girls do for festivals — braids, and red and blue ribbons with red roses. My legs made a pleasant swishing sound that came from mother's silk stockings rubbing together.

There is a feeling you get when you're dressed to go someplace grand — your outside is so beautiful that it seeps in through your skin. You become kind, generous, witty, and with the dazzle of your smile momentarily blinding your family, you are a queen. I graciously accepted the bouquets of praise they tossed at me.

Nessa wanted me to bring her a jelly cookie, and Rachel begged that I remember *all* the dresses. Jake insisted that I get to the stable for a look at the baron's new black horse from Moscow that all the boys were talking about. My mother cautioned me to behave myself. Why wouldn't I?

The midday sun beat down on our kolyaska, its leather hood pushed back to give it a sportier look. I sat up in the driver's seat with Cousin Avram, who fancied himself a horseman and always drove his own carriage. The baron's estate covered about 1,000 acres — mostly wheat and sugar beets. Beside the road that wound through the grounds the peasants knelt to thin and weed the rows of young beets, one worker for every two rows and each row with its own child worker. Girls my age, each with a water bucket and tube attachment, watered the kneeling workers by sticking the tube in their mouths. The beet fields gave way to the dark green of the nobleman's orchards. Bunches of deep-red cherries hung from the trees by the side of the road. The cherry-vodka liqueur bottled on the estate was famous throughout the province.

The lane to the mansion was lined with pines so tall and thick they blocked the view of the grounds. We drove under a green iron arch that bore the Tretyakov coat of arms, a tree with one branch flowering into the head of a wolf, another into the head of a lamb. "Tproo," called Avram, and the horses stopped.

The garden party sprawled over the wide brick terrace to the lawn below, where the mousey-looking Tatiana received her guests in a wicker chair festooned with daisy wreaths. As instructed, I handed her the gift — perfume from France — "La Lune Bleu." The box had no smell. I had sniffed the entire surface hoping for the odor of Paris. A gentleman in a gray-striped suit called to Cousin Avram, "Mr. Vorontsov, come and tell me about the Priluki matter." With a pat on by braids and a "Have fun, little one," he left me, his admission ticket, standing on the terrace next to a pot of petunias.

I wished he had taken me with him; I would rather have listened to his business conversation and belonged to somebody than to be alone. I stationed myself under a large poplar where I had a good view of the house and garden, hoping to see my friends, Nikon and Marusya. The terrace was set with two serving tables covered in white damask. Spread under them were matching red carpets woven with pink cabbage roses. A little boy in a sailor suit leaned over the back of a white wrought-iron bench, systematically denuding a fern. The number of bare strands showed he must have been at it for a long time. Servants carrying platters of food ran in and out the door of the white mansion with the high red roof. But the Troyans were not among the guests who laughed and talked together, at ease on the nobleman's terrace.

From somewhere near the summerhouse came the clink of croquet mallets. Blue-green peacocks swaggered across the lawn, showing off their brilliant tail fans, bending their slender necks into the beds of red petunias. A group of young mothers, twirling their silk parasols, kept an eye on their infants as they toddled and fell in the grass. I smiled and tried to look as though I belonged.

I was dressed right, but I knew I was different. I was a stranger to the boys paddling rowboats in the pond and the giggling girls who held hands and paraded along the shore. I couldn't go running to my mother like the little boy in the sailor suit when he fell off the bench. My family, though they didn't look much different from these people, wasn't rich enough to be part of Dmitrovka society and probably never would be, because if you were Jewish you had to be extra rich. And even then, like Cousin Avram, no matter how hard you tried, you still never really belonged. Maybe part of it was not having land. Though some Jewish people got around the law and owned property, no Jews I had ever heard of owned great estates, or even small ones. Land, money, the Russian Orthodox religion — I would never be like these people.

The sound of a hand organ, tinny and gay, broke into my thoughts. The organ-grinder nodded to me. His sad little monkey, all dressed up in a satin suit, curly tail poking out behind him, tried to hide himself in his master's jacket. I wished I could do the same.

Then I spotted Marusya walking down the summer-house steps. She did a little pirouette and ran to me, her smile dousing my feeling of being the only one at the party who didn't know anyone else. We wandered off in the direction of the sweet table.

Something red and purple streaked by. The monkey had gotten away. A group of children charged after the organ-grinder and we joined them. You didn't have to know anyone to play this game; it felt good to be a part of that well-dressed throng. Then through a grove of birches I caught a glimpse of a black horse. It must have been the one Jake wanted me to see, and I called to Marusya, who followed me into the trees. The horse turned out to be a swaybacked nag whose only resemblance to the baron's racehorse was his membership in the species Equus caballus. So we ran off in the direction of the shouts but found only more trees and more bushes. We were lost somewhere in the baron's gardens, in a patch of wild strawberries. Without a word, we sat down and began to eat.

"What are you girls doing?"

In our scramble to get up we cracked heads. The raspy edge of the voice alarmed us.

Klym Sereda ran his eyes down Marusya, then me. His lips slid into a smile. Mean, lightning-bolt lines fanned out from the bridge of his snub nose. He looked different somehow. Shorter. Then I realized his back was hunched over, as if he were suddenly old. His jacket, the kind they sold in the dry goods store, was too small for him and his wrist hung out as he stretched his arm toward Marusya.

The knout attached to his belt made an unfriendly stripe down his pant leg.

"Yes. The name day. I've been celebrating, too." He staggered, then turned and looked at me as if he were trying to see under my skin. His hand circled my neck, kneading at it like a persistent cat.

"Let go!"

The kneading stopped; he cupped his hand where his left ear ought to be. "Eh? Try to look pretty. Like your tall friend here. Rich people's children need to learn manners, too."

"You'd better take us to the party or the baron will be angry with you," I said. "Immediately." A lion, yes. My eyes never left his. I could hear Marusya's deep, astonished breath. He shook his head as if he had water in his ears, then ran a big hand down his face, pulling at his nose.

"Yes. I know how to treat young ladies. Do you think I'm just a moujik? I'm the overseer to Baron Tretyakov." He bowed stiffly. "Here, I will take you." He tried to link arms with us.

"No. You walk ahead," I told him.

"Yes, of course." His smile had nothing to do with happiness — it was simply an arrangement of skin and teeth. Soon we heard party noises and dashed ahead to hide among the pastel dresses.

The roses. The roses.
The young girls are sweeter.
The spring turns to summer,

The daffodils to pansies,
The lilacs to goldenrod.

A group of peasant girls, their white blouses embroidered in red flowers, red ribbons streaming from their coiled braids, swayed as they sang. A double-chinned babushkaed servingwoman passed a bowl of cherries. But Klym Sereda's spell hung over the party. He was like a wicked host who enticed the children with fun and sweets in order to cook them for dinner.

"That man — he's the murderer. Klym Sereda. The one . . ." Before I could tell Marusya any more, Cousin Avram had come to collect me. "Find out about him," I called to her as I took his arm and went off to pay a farewell tribute to the baron and Tatiana.

8

Cousin Avram and I had been friends ever since I could remember. According to my parents, his own children, who were away at school most of the year, wrote their father only to ask for a better horse or a bigger allowance. So he told me what he would like to tell them, "how the world works." "Business pulls the cart; money greases the wheels." "No risk, no gain." He sighed. "I wish you were a boy. None of my sons gives a fig for business. All they care about is spending."

My cousin was an agreeable man who, unlike most grown-ups, made me feel important because he really heard what I said. Maybe that's why other people liked him, too — and they did. Papa called him "a gymnast of high society — when it comes to making the right friends, his timing and balance are perfect." Our noisy Kagan relatives spoke of him reverently, always asking about his health, and when they met him at our house they reined in their boisterous ways and became ladies and gentlemen like him and Cousin Anna.

"Don't you look lovely. Sit down."

We were in his office in the bank where my brother and the Troyans had sent me to talk to him. The twins had quizzed their father about Klym Sereda. They found out the baron spent too much time in Moscow racing horses and dancing at his wife's parties. The house-servants on the estate stole from him, and the yield from his fields was down 20 percent. And everyone knew that a good share of the estate's proceeds went directly into the foreman's pocket — everyone but the baron, who, being from an ancient family whose title was bestowed by Catherine the Great, didn't care to bother his head with bookkeeping.

Jake, the Troyans, and I had decided that the way to bring Sereda to the law was tell the baron about the murder. Anyone who was as vain about his title as the baron wouldn't want to dishonor it by having a criminal run his affairs. And who would be the best person to inform on Sereda? Avram Vorontsov, the banker to the Tretyakov fortune.

I loved Avram's office. You had to go upstairs, past three men in dark coats who sat on stools, their pens scratching at the heavy white paper, down the narrow, windowless hall to the small door at the end. The room where my cousin sat behind his polished walnut desk was like the inside of a strongbox, dark and quiet and filled with things that glittered and glowed — an antique silver letter opener with an embossed handle, a pearl in a glass paperweight given him "in gratitude," a gold nugget from an "investment" in Siberia.

He raised his hands over his desk and beamed like the

rabbi calling on God's countenance to shine over his congregation. "What can I do for you?" He took a cigar from an inlaid box, clipped off the end, and tapped it smartly. The first puff glowed a perfect circle. From time to time a smoke ring slid from his mouth as he listened to my story of the murder in the cornfield and finally to my plea that he intercede with the baron.

He sat silently for what seemed like a long time. We stared at each other. He looked away. There was a knock on the door and one of the men in dark coats came in with some papers for him to sign. The man, who was so pale it crossed my mind that he lived somewhere in a dark corner of the bank, hummed under his breath as he waited for Avram to read through the papers.

"Libby, my dear child," he said after the man left, "did you know I'm only the baron's number two banker? Number one is in Moscow. But I'm working on it." A corner of his mouth turned up.

I took a deep breath. The room smelled of cigar smoke and cloves.

"It's an unhappy surprise for a man to find he's put his trust where he shouldn't have. He feels like a fool, so he acts like one. What does he do? He takes his humiliation out on the informant. I'm sure you see where that puts me."

I didn't see at all.

"Sereda has not actually harmed you or your family — which is also my family. Yes, he killed a peasant. But the peasants, they have arguments. Someone gets killed. It happens."

"Klym Sereda murdered a man. I saw him." I stood up.
"What I saw is in me now."

He took my hand and did something no one had ever done before. He kissed it.

"Libby, it's just not good business. Pretend it never happened. What 'they' do is no concern of ours."

To the Baron Nicholas Tretyakov
Your Excellency,

We feel it our duty to inform you of the heinous behavior of your foreman, one Klym Sereda. On the morning of June 12, he beat a moujik, Stepan Marchenko, to death in the cornfield of the white house that belonged to the governor of Cernigov province. He also drinks on the job and mistreats your workers. This is why your crop yield is off twenty percent.

We are sure that a man of noble character such as yourself would not want an execrable person in his employ — a person who would dishonor the House of Tretyakov. We are also positive that you would want to take him to the police so that justice can be done.

We respectfully request that you satisfy yourself of this matter by questioning Klym Sereda. We know your wisdom will immediately perceive his guilt.

We are respectfully and humbly,
YOUR FRIENDS

61

Just two days after my meeting with my cousin, Jake left this letter in the baron's onion-domed mailbox. When the nobleman was away, the house steward would put all the mail on the Moscow train. We found this out from Mitya, who was the steward's son.

The days bumped and dragged as if they were pulled by a tinker's cart. Then, after a week passed, the diphtheria came to Dmitrovka, though not to our home.

We were sentenced to house arrest. We sat in the stifling rooms and banged on the piano, drank lemonade, played statues and iks-mics-driks, read till our eyes crossed, and generally got on each other's nerves.

We spent a lot of time in the parlor, a place that was usually off limits. All our relatives had a room like it, stiff, seldom used, with dark, claw-footed furniture that barked your shins, and air that was musty from hanging undisturbed for days at a time. We had to be careful of things — the glass swan bowl full of dried violets, the gilt Sevres vase, a wedding present from Avram and Anna. No matter how long we spent there, it never felt like part of our house.

The only useful object in the room was the piano that sat between the two big windows looking out toward the road. It was an upright, made out of a reddish wood with a black grain; four round columns held up the keyboard part. When Sarah was little she thought the brass pedals that poked out of the bottom belonged to a three-footed animal who lived inside and sang when you pushed on his teeth. Papa was the only one who played, though he was teaching Nessa. Early in the morning, through the closed door, we would hear the scales and our father's patient tones, "E E D D. Play what you read, child."

Sprawled out on the slick brocade sofa, with the door locked and the windows open a forbidden crack, Jake and I had long talks about life in general and our lives in particular. He told me that if Papa didn't take us to America, he was going to run away and emigrate when he was eighteen. Dmitrovka without my brother was too painful for me to contemplate. He begged me for the tenth time to take him to the cornfield to the scene of the murder. As always I answered, "We'll see." I wasn't ready to go back there yet. We spoke of the reason for the closed windows, Mama's Germ Theory. To Mother, fresh air during an epidemic was an enemy whose constant assault upon one's house and loved ones must be met with the sternest measures. Closed windows, hurried exits and entrances, imprisonment for the children, the very people the airborne germs were looking for. Part and parcel of the theory was the idea that the sun heats up the offending microbes, making the days riskier than the nights. There are other parts of it. I'm not sure I understand it all. It's a very complicated theory.

The day Jake told me about Klym Sereda and the horses we forgot to lock the door and Mama, her hands dripping soapsuds, her nose scenting fresh germs, dashed in from the kitchen, slammed the window shut, and ran out without a word. Jake and I were trying to figure out how a man as bad as Sereda could become an overseer for a baron. "Mitya says he's a different person around the horses." The stableboy told him that Sereda's voice gets soft and sweet when he talks to the horses; he calls them names like "Little Ballerina" and "Earthmover." He brings them sugar lumps from the kitchen. And once Mitya watched with him while he sat up all night with a sick mare. He actually sang her a lullaby.

On the afternoon of the next day I was reading in the parlor. The room was full of heat and light, but the heat didn't warm you, it smothered, and the light didn't cheer you, it glared.

I heard a scratching noise; a branch with a piece of paper stuck on it was clawing at the window. Germs or no germs, I threw it open and gulped the air. Olga, our cook, who had been home with her husband and two little girls during the epidemic, held the other end of the branch. I brought the note to my mother, who was in the kitchen hoisting a steaming cow's tongue from a kettle.

Dear Mrs. Kagan,

My Natasha has died of the fever. You have some little dresses packed away in the cedar chest. Might I have the blue one with the scalloped apron to bury my child in? May God bless you.

Olga

Tears welled in my mother's eyes as she scanned the crumpled piece of paper. "Wash your hands from the note. Scrub them!" she ordered.

Mama found the dress and waved it out the window. Olga raised her stick, and Mother tied the little blue sleeves to the branch. Dropping to her knees, our cook kissed an icon and made the sign of the cross.

Later that afternoon, as I sat in my room, the funeral procession went by our house. It reminded me of the "play funerals" Nessa and Rachel loved to give for their dolls — the tiny coffin, the other children, Olga's nephews and nieces, marching along beside it. Two bearded priests in their shroudlike robes, each swinging a glowing icon led the column to the graveyard about a half mile from our house. A peasant family, a mother, father, and small boy walked in the opposite direction, toward town. The father stopped and took off his cap; the mother covered her child's face with one hand and crossed herself with the other.

The blue dress that the dead Natasha wore had once been mine, my party dress. It made me feel cold and hollow as a hay straw to think of it covering that small, still body—the last clothing she would ever wear. As I sat wondering if there was diphtheria in America, Grandma came in to sit with me and told a story she had told many times before.

My mother's little brothers, who would have been my uncles, had died of diphtheria when they were very small children. David, the five-year-old, could read like a child of ten, while the younger one, Daniel, had the disposition of an angel. There had been no doctor in the town of Saray, only a felsher. Most felshers had no real medical training; they learned from old books and folk tales or from other felshers. He came to see Daniel and David; he touched the babies' hot foreheads and looked at their red throats. "I'm going to try something new here. Don't give them any water." Oh, how they begged for a drink. David promised my mother, his sister, he would do her chores when he got well, if she would just give him water, but she wasn't allowed to. Both boys died on the same night.

Their father, my grandfather, put on his coat and went on a mission. He knocked at every door in Saray in the middle of that night. "If your children are stricken, give them water! Mine died. They burned up."

On the fifteenth day, a Wednesday, market day, my mother declared the epidemic officially over. Only three people had died — Natasha and two other babies. That morning, as Jake and I set out for the market square where we knew we would find Nikon and Marusya, everything looked new to me. Across the street the birch trunks seemed as if they'd been whitewashed. The smell of fresh-cut hay floated in the air. Some peasants were tying bundles of straw for a roofless hut that gaped open to the sky. A slat-sided cart crowded with geese trundled by, while a moujik, his trousers tucked into his baggy boots, hurried past with a squealing pig under his arm. Wagons of hay, watermelons, turnips, and cabbage jolted down the dusty road to town.

Some younger children played king-of-the-palace in the little field next to the blacksmith's shop. "What do you wish, prince?" "The prince wants the princess in the palace." As we passed the jail, three soldiers stepped out, their belts and boots shining in the morning sun. The soapsuds in the Little-River-Without-a-Name told us that we had arrived at the old wooden bridge that led to the main part of town, for it was on the other side of the bridge that the peasant women scrubbed their clothes on the great flat stones that had been spread there by their ancestors generations ago. They slapped at the rocks with their wet shirts and laughed and gossiped the morning away.

In the center of Dmitrovka, on the street of the market square, all the buildings were of brick — the barber shop, the government school, the post office. And sandwiched in between the seltzer store and the kerosene shop was the inn with the sign that I'd loved since I was a little girl. Swinging from a pole, carved and painted to giant-sized perfection were a steaming samovar, a half glass of tea, and a white plate. On the plate sat a piece of red salami and a purple onion.

Six days a week the market square was empty except for the rusty water pump and the firebell. On the seventh day it was thronged with sellers, their goods and animals, and buyers, who moved from stall to stall hunting for the best bargains. Avoiding Makar, the street sweeper, as he stirred up the dust with his crooked broom, we crossed the road into the square. I immediately helped myself to a cottage cheese varenky from a folding table manned by an old fellow in a stained apron. Jake, who carried the money, sighed and paid him. "We're not here to fill your stomach. We're looking for the twins, remember?" A red-haired Jewish man, his cap askew, called to us to see his bolts of "first quality cloth," then, as we passed him by, pounded his chest in mock despair. A peasant woman, her many chins resting on her bosom, squatted beside her

67

basket of carrots, munching on one of her wares. She stuck the half-eaten carrot under my brother's nose, cackling as he pushed it away.

The noises wove themselves into our hum, but if I thought about it I could separate them, the hand-clap signaling the closing of a deal, the peddlers chanting their wares, the animals squealing for their freedom. I was aware of a new sound, the trill of a flute. Jake and I smiled at each other and followed the music through the crowd to Nikon and Marusya, who were listening to a boy demonstrate the wooden flutes he was selling from a cart filled with cabbages, strawberries, and flutes.

They wanted to go someplace quiet. They had a lot to tell us. But first Marusya asked that we go to our corn-field to see where the murder had taken place. If Jake hadn't been in the house with me the past two weeks, I would have thought he put her up to it. I had been back to pick corn but had kept to the edges of the field. I really didn't want to see that place again — maybe I wouldn't even remember the exact spot — but to be a coward in front of my friends — that was worse, so I agreed.

When I had gone back before I always tried to keep Stepan Marchenko, the dead man, out of my mind, but it didn't work. This time, as we entered the field, the stalks taller now, the corn past its prime, I could hear his ghost in the breeze that rustled the leaves; I could feel it in the earth under my feet. I held my brother's arm; none of us said a word. When I got to what looked like the place, I stood and told them again, in the presence of the ghost, of his murder. As I heard myself speak, I realized that

what I was saying was just words and that a man was dead
forever — whether Klym Sereda was brought to justice
or not, not justice, not revenge, not words could bring a
dead man back to life, so what good were they?

When I finished my story, everyone was silent. Even
the crow on a nearby stalk sat motionless, his head cocked,
his beak half open, listening. The breeze had stopped. The
only sound was a yellow grasshopper clicking his way
down the row.

Nikon took up his flute and began to play a mournful
tune. I did not know the live Stepan Marchenko. I only
knew him dead, so I couldn't mourn him, yet I couldn't
rid myself of him. The flute playing comforted me.

Nikon, still playing the bushtree flute, led the way to our
pond where we sat on rocks that were large and flat like
the ones the peasant women used to wash their clothes.
There were no trees around the pond, only cattails and
the small red willow bushes. The open space felt good
after the dense green of the cornfield.

"The baron never got the letter — Sereda did," was
how Nikon began his tale.

Mrs. Troyan, with no theory to guide her, had released
Nikon and Marusya from quarantine two days before we
were let out. They hadn't even bothered to come by our
house, familiar as they were with Mama's germ warfare.
And since the oradnick hadn't mentioned a word about
Klym, Nikon went to see Mitya.

"It's because they're crooked as hairpins over there at
the baron's," said Marusya, her high voice indignant.

It seemed that the house servants were in the habit of steaming open the baron's mail before they sent it off to Moscow.

"My father likes to know everything that's happening around here," Mitya had told Nikon. "We have a pretty good setup at Tretyakov's, and, well, you can't be too careful. Don't say I told you."

Nikon reassured him with a fellow horseman's pledge and a pouch of tobacco.

At first Mitya's father was going to burn the letter, reasoning that if the baron started asking questions about Sereda, he might move his inquiry right through the front door of the house. But instead he handed Klym the letter on the same silver platter he used to bring the baron his morning mail. It could be helpful to have the foreman in his debt.

Klym was so grateful, he fell to his knees and sobbed out his thanks.

I watched Nikon as he told the story, tilting his head, looking out from under his thick eyelashes the way he always does when he talks about something important. His dark eyes glinted yellow, then green.

Jake and the twins speculated as to whether Klym would suspect the Kagans, since the letter mentioned our house. They invented crazy tricks to lure the murderer into a confession. They conjured up impossible circumstances that would expose his villainy in public.

"What are you talking about?" I could contain myself no longer. "You sound as crazy as old Grisha. And besides, bringing Klym to justice won't do a thing for the dead man and it could bring trouble for us. Papa's right. Let's forget about it."

You could have cut their surprise with a bread knife. "But you're the one . . ." "You *sound* like Papa."

Nikon was quiet at first. There is a stillness about him. He thinks before he talks. "To do nothing — it would be wrong. There is an order to things," he finally said.

"I don't understand. All I know is that if we *could* do something, which we can't, it wouldn't matter anyway."

A lock of black hair fell across Nikon's forehead. He brushed it away impatiently. "It would matter. That's what I mean about an order to things. People — we all — have a duty to keep things right. We know about a murder. The killer has to be punished so he won't kill someone again. Good and evil. If we help good win out, the world will be better. In order." He had gotten off his rock and stood, the pond behind him, speaking earnestly and formally, the way his father did when he made a speech at a town ceremony.

The others took up his theme. We *had* to do it. We *could* do it. They spoke to me like my conscience. And so my discouragement was forgotten, my spirit revived.

Marusya went home to a tea with her mother; Jake went off reluctantly to soak paper in the factory, a smelly, messy job. Nikon and I made our way to the beehives at the edge of the cherry orchard. On our way, we stopped at a bottom-picked tree and clambered into the highest of the silvery-maroon limbs, stuffing our mouths and pockets with the smooth, round fruit, knowing as does every child in Dmitrovka, that the sweetest cherries grow at the top of the tree. At the wicker beehives I watched Nikon, who had an understanding with the bees, edge into their midst, drop his shoulders, relax his body, and stand patiently until they ignored him as if he were a tree trunk or a statue of a boy. Someday maybe I would try it, if I could summon up the patience.

It began to rain, a hard downpour, and we ran through the orchard, past the cellar door, the pump, and the woodpile, to the shelter of my father's hotel. It wasn't really a hotel, just a large, open room that had been added on to the west side of the house near the factory by the governor's wife. As she liked her privacy, it had no connecting door to the main house.

There had been two groups of people in constant attendance at the governor's, those who came to *ask* for something — a better road to their town, a job for a brother-in-law, a new church bell for Sunday mornings. And there were officials from Kiev and Moscow who came to *tell* him something — how to run the schools, the way to catch more criminals, that he needed to collect higher taxes for the Tsar.

Dmitrovka had no inn at that time, and there was not enough room in the house for all the petitioners and all the agents of the Tsar, so a guest room was built, all of wood, about thirty feet long and twelve feet wide, with three-foot shelves around the walls. With the addition of comforters and pillows, the shelves made excellent beds.

My father also had a perfect use for those shelves. He boarded peasants while they waited the few days it took to process their wool. We children had great games and meetings in the hotel during the off seasons, in spite of the faint smell of wet wool that clung to the walls.

We threw open the latch on the planked door and ran in. Our laughter, hollow in the big empty room, surprised us into silence. We dried ourselves on a tattered nightshirt we found crumpled and forgotten in a corner. The dull light that came from the windows at either end of the room yellowed the birch walls and floors, while the wet wool smell, heightened by the dampness, lay heavy in the air.

The rain drummed the roof as the two of us stretched out head to head, in opposite directions on the shelf-beds. As we stared at the ceiling of rough-hewn birch logs, I felt Nikon's head touching mine.

"Sereda is going to come nosing around. This house is the only clue he has as to who wrote the letter. He's got to follow it up. Try and stay with Jake — or anyone. Just don't be alone."

Somehow what he was saying didn't frighten me. All I could think of was his closeness.

"I don't want anything to happen to you. I like you too much. You . . . I never know what you're going to do next."

I couldn't have answered if I'd wanted to — it felt as if someone had just sat on my chest. No longer could I see the knotty ceiling logs. Even though he hadn't moved, Nikon's face, his square chin with the cleft in it, his straight black eyebrows, had replaced them.

Suddenly the door flew open, and we sat up. Trying to

squeeze in at the same time were Papa, Klym Sereda, and the rain.

"Nobody. So I see," said Klym Sereda. He looked at me as if I were nobody, then pulled off his cap and wiped his face on his sleeve. He squinted his pale-blue eyes; his lips stiffened into a mean line.

"There is no peasant here," my father said sternly.

Sereda leaned close to me. Gray raindrops nestled in his beard; I tried not to look at the place where his ear ought to be. "Has anyone been here besides you?"

"No. No one."

Nikon stood in front of me. "No one," he said, a little louder than he meant to.

"What are you doing at this house? You shouldn't be here," Sereda said, his tone half angry, half respectful, the chilly eyes flickering from Nikon to me.

"My father knows I'm here." Nikon set his hands on his hips. He was taller than Sereda by a head.

"This is my daughter. She knows nothing about your runaway," my father said.

"So. What *does* she know about?" asked Klym Sereda as he backed out into the rain.

9

The rest of the summer we waited for the whip to crack. But the August days bloomed into goldenrod, asters, and longer nights. We stayed together, riding horses to the old stone lookout tower halfway to Konotop, swimming in the warm, muddy pond behind the wall. I helped out around the house, milking the cows with Old Crazy Boris, who clicked his heels and waltzed around the barn in time to his own mysterious music. I ironed my mother's sheer white blouses that Natalka always burned, and learned to prepare some of Olga's specialties — radish-honey preserves, and the tart, lemony sand cakes.

Doing mindless tasks gave me time to think — about Nikon — we hadn't talked alone since the hotel — but most of all about Klym Sereda. The more I thought about him, the angrier I got. We were all afraid — we children, hoping he wouldn't harm us, and my parents and Cousin Avram, fearing for different reasons to turn him in. We had to walk carefully, yet we had done nothing. It was as if *we* were paying for *his* crime.

We ate our way through the orchard, the peaches tastier than ever, the four old pear trees fruiting as if they were young again. The beauty of the season, heightened by the sharp length of the Ukrainian winters, lulled us into a growing feeling of security.

Soon it was time to harvest the little pickling cucumbers, a task I've done every year since I was five. Grandma showed me how to pickle and now it was something we always did together. One of the reasons I like it so much is that she always tells me stories. But this year, she was strangely silent.

The morning after the harvest was in, Grandma and I carried the first hemp bags of cucumbers down the 15 bowed wooden steps into the root cellar, which stood about 20 feet from the house. The slanted roof, covered with squares of well-kept sod could barely be seen by someone drawing water from the pump outside the kitchen. I always felt immediately invisible when I entered the door of the cellar.

The room, with its hard dirt walls and floors, was like a clover-shaped cave. Its ceiling, about seven feet high, had a little chimney-pipe opening for ventilation, with a cap to protect it from the rain and snow. All year round the temperature was the same early autumn cool; it was a perfect storage place for all kinds of food.

I knew the contents of the cellar by heart. At the bottom of the stairs on the right, the nearest barrel to the door, were the sour red beets, whose brine we mixed with warm water to wash our hair. Next came the "combined barrel" containing layers of cucumbers, tomatoes, cabbages, apples, and carrots soaking in salt water and spices. Milk and cheese were in the clover leaf to the left while bins of winter apples and pears, onions, radishes, and other vegetables lined the walls of the remaining alcoves.

Grandma and I dropped the fresh cucumbers into a barrel of garlic brine. She had her sleeves rolled up, exposing the thin, white skin on the undersides of her arms. The blue veins knotted as she lifted each bag.

"Grandma, why can't we make things in our lives turn out the way they should? The way we want?"

She looked at me sharply. "Why do you ask? Does it have to do with that Sereda fellow?"

"I just want to know."

"Well, sometimes you can and other times you can't. But you must *always* try. Without a rider how does the horse know where to go?" She laughed. "Let me tell you a story about that — how I played a game with God and won."

Though I had heard the story many times before, each time she told it was like the first time.

"You know about my little boys who died? Your uncles, David and Daniel?"

I nodded.

Grandma put her hands to her cheeks, pushing, pushing.

"After they died I decided that I had to do something. Something to keep your mother from dying. She was all I had left.

"So I got the idea of playing a game with God. There

was a poor family in Saray whose eight children lived through all the epidemics. I made a deal with them. I would take your mother — she was seven years old — to their house in the morning, with enough food for the day. 'Here. Here is your child. Take her back,' I would say. And the woman would say to me, 'Good. Give me back my child. None of *my* children die.'

"Bayla would stay all day, helping the woman pull goose feathers — that was how she earned her living — and helping with the children. In the evening I would go back to that shabby house and ask, 'Please lend me your child for the night.' The answer was always the same, 'You may take her. *My* children don't die.'

"We did that for five years." Grandma's face lit up in a triumphant smile. "Until we left for Dmitrovka. I won. My child lived. But it's strange. Ever since then we don't really understand each other. All those years, she was another woman's child."

Grandma, who was not an affectionate woman, put her arms around me, then held me at arm's length, looking into my face as if for the answer to an important question.

"But she's alive. And you're alive," she said. "And because I took matters into my own hands like that, some other lives got changed around, too."

I knew what was coming. The next story went with the first, like garlic with dill.

"You remember what the woman's husband did for a living?"

"He was a chopper."

A chopper was a grabber. In those days the local rabbi

was commanded to produce a certain number of Jewish men to serve in the army. He had to come up with his quota, or there was trouble for the Jews. The chopper worked for the rabbi. He grabbed young Jewish men who were unlucky enough to walk the streets of a strange town during the time when the Tsar put out a call for soldiers.

"Well, one day your mother was left alone in the house. She sat in front of a huge pile of feathers, pulling the soft part and tossing away the spine. She heard a noise coming from the top of the big brick oven. It got louder and louder. It sounded like someone groaning.

"Bayla was only eight, but she was smart. Like you." Grandma flicked my shoulder. "She knew the profession of her daily host, so quick as a bird, she hopped up on the stove. And what do you think she saw?" Grandma's eyes snapped. "A handsome, well-dressed Jewish boy tied up with ropes. A fine present for the Tsar's army.

"Bayla ran home as fast as she could. When her father heard the story I thought he was going to have some kind of attack. But he was young and strong then, and he tossed her up on his horse, jumped on behind her, and galloped off to rescue the young man.

"But the chopper couldn't be bought off. 'I've told the authorities I have something for them,' he said. 'I'll lose my job if I let the boy go.'

"What could your grandfather do? He couldn't go to the police." Raising her eyebrows, she stopped and waggled a finger at me. "But then he got an idea. It just so happened the feather-puller and the chopper had a daughter of marriageable age. So Grandpa had a conference with the boy on the oven. What did he think about his freedom in exchange for marrying these poor people's daughter? Well, he jumped at the chance. Grandpa said it probably didn't hurt that he had noticed the beautiful dark eyes of Rivka, the oldest girl in the family.

"What a match! He was the son of wealthy people from a neighboring village. He got fooled by the liberal ways of Tsar Alexander the Second and carelessly walked through Saray just when the chopper needed to fill an order.

"So your grandpa hired a balagole and returned with the boy's father, who said yes to anything that would free his son.

"But that chopper! He wouldn't give in until the rich man signed a paper releasing the bride-to-be from the obligation of the marriage dowry. And more! He had the nerve to insist that the wedding take place right then and there. He didn't trust anyone. Maybe it's because his own business was such a sneaky one.

"The end of the story is this: About a year and a half later a red ribboned sledge pulled up in front of the little house of the chopper and the feather-puller. In it, wrapped in furs, were the beautiful, dark-eyed Rivka, her handsome husband, and their healthy, golden-haired baby girl come to visit the family of the young wife and mother."

I sat in the cool quiet letting the rhythms of the story wash over me. "The beautiful dark eyes of Rivka." "My children don't die."

Grandma stared off into the shadows of the cellar, back into the time when my mother was a little girl, and her husband, my grandfather, was alive and strong, and she was in charge of a house the way Mama is now.

Grandma pushed at her cheeks, the way she always did when she told a story. "So, Libby, if you want things to come out in a certain way, you have to fight." Again she put her hands on my shoulders, holding me off at arm's length, but so tenderly it could have been another embrace. "However, my dear — it doesn't always work."

At the height of the baron's harvest, we went back to school. The peasant children, who went to government schools, were still helping their families in the fields. Jake was to go to work in our factory, keeping the machines in order. In the evenings he would study with a private tutor. Nikon went to a small gymnasium for the wealthier boys, while Marusya attended a church school for young ladies. I joined my sisters at Miss Minna Illichna's school for Jewish girls, which she held in the small house that had belonged to her mother. This meant, of course, that Marusya and I had to put up with our annual winter separation.

But after school, when she wasn't dancing, and always on the weekends, we spent time together making gigantic snow forts and sledding down the wooden ice slide that they built every winter by the Little-River-Without-a-Name. The slide, our favorite winter entertainment, was 20 or 25 feet tall, a wooden platform supported by tree trunks with a tree-trunk ladder. The surface was blocks of ice that the children kept in shape by bringing snow and pouring water on it. We carved little sleds out of ice, filled them with straw, bored a hole at one end for a rope, and sped down faster than a runaway horse. We skated for hours on the pond and warmed ourselves with cups of hot chocolate and long talks that turned, on my part, around Nikon, and whatever novel I was reading, on hers, the famous young dancers with the Imperial Ballet, Anna Pavlova, Tamara Karsovina, and her own chances of convincing her parents to allow her to apply to the Kiev Academy of Dance.

By December, the ice and snow of winter had shrunk the events of summer into something small and far away.

10

◇ ◇ ◇

"Could we do any better in America?"

Cousin Avram waved his arm around his dining room. The walls were covered in dusky rose silk. The backs and seats of the carved chairs were needlepointed in the design of an old fashioned garden. The carpet was French, as were the tapestries on which elegant men and women picnicked in a forest.

"I don't see how," I said.

Papa had been going on about taking the family to America. It was his dream, and he had been mentioning it more often this past year. When he invited Avram and his family to come with us, my cousin gave him that look he usually saves for eccentrics.

"You could have a bigger bank in America," my father said.

"I can have a bigger bank here."

"But it's so big already," put in Cousin Anna, and we all laughed. Even she laughed as she handed around more

83

of the tiny blini. Cousin Anna always made us feel good. She was a sweet, blonde, mild woman who ate milk toast for her digestion. She walked with a slight limp, and when I was little I used to ask her how she got it. One time she said her nurse dropped her when she was a baby and another that she was born that way, while only last year she told me she had been cured at the age of 16 of a terrible crippling disease by a famous doctor from France who, upon her recovery, had asked for her hand in marriage. I don't think she remembered herself. Whenever she went out on the streets, she carried a silken parasol; a servant, usually holding a wooden-handled shopping bag, walked behind her.

Both she and Avram were born to the life they lived, coming from wealthy families that had considered themselves Russian for many generations. The Vorontsov sons had always gone to Russian gymnasiums in Kiev and university in Moscow, just as they were now. Their only daughter, Katya, who was two years older than I, stayed with a distant relative in Kiev, where she was entertained at the best houses. The Vorontsovs looked down their noses at most of the other Jewish families in town, preferring the society of prominent gentiles. And the key to the front door of their bank seemed to unlock the doors and hearts of whomever it was they wanted to know.

The reason why they considered themselves Russian, at least according to the story we've always been told about the name Vorontsov, my mother's maiden name, goes like this: Some two hundred years ago in the time of Catherine the Great, an ancestor of ours was a financial advisor to the Queen. Now, Catherine was a busy ruler, grabbing up thousands of acres along the borders and building over one hundred new towns, so she needed money to pay her soldiers and her architects.

Back then, most Jews didn't have last names. They were called by their occupations — Jacob the Tailor, or by their ancestors, David ben (son of) Abraham, or by where they lived, Mordecai of Priluki. The empress was so pleased with my ancestor's shrewd financial advice that she bestowed on him the last name of one of her lovers, Vorontsov. To Cousin Avram's way of thinking, the name cast a more favorable light than even his three crystal chandeliers.

Two young, solemn-faced girls came in balancing silver trays. Rachel and Nessa sat with their mouths open, not for the food, but for the ceremony — and for the uniforms, black dresses with white, ruffled aprons, high, starched collars, and little butterfly caps. A tiny moist cloud appeared in front of Cousin Anna. It was the salmon sighing as she broke into the flaky pastry that surrounded it.

"Oh, a kulebiaka," I said, in spite of myself. "That's made with onions and dill, mushrooms, rice, and lemon juice."

Cousin Anna shrugged and smiled.

"It's a blessing she can cook," my mother said.

I may be the dunce of the sewing circle, but in the kitchen I feel like Catherine the Great. My potato kugels

are lighter than anyone else's. (Old potatoes work best.)
On Friday nights, my challah rises to unheard-of heights.
(It's in the kneading.)

I have, since I was about eight, the ability to tell just
from the tasting what goes into a certain dish. And I am
the only child in my family who always tries every new
food — even things that are mushy, stringy, or liver-
colored. A long time ago when I started going to Olga's to
play with her daughters, I coaxed her into letting me taste
the forbidden pork, her spicy sausage and crackling roasts.
There was no tradition strong enough to thwart my
curiosity about food.

The Vorontsovs didn't keep kosher and their dinners
were the best I've ever eaten. Maybe that was the reason.
They cooked dairy and meat in the same pots and served
them on the same plates at the same time, but for us they
separated them, keeping a kosher appearance. My parents
couldn't imagine abandoning the dietary laws of our ancestors, but they accepted the Vorontsovs' occasional sum-
mons to dinner, understanding that the meal would *look*
kosher and we should not ask to inspect the kitchen. However, even at the Vorontsovs, pork was still forbidden.

The next course was a soup served from a gold-leafed
tureen. It was a beet broth with vegetables and diced
meat. I leaned and sniffed: dill and leeks, garlic, cabbage,
and something I couldn't identify. I watched the nine
descendants of that ancient and respected Vorontsov who
told the queen how to use her money eat their soup —
and each and every one of them, their faces sober, their
spoons tilted just so, approached each mouthful with a

refinement that did him honor. I tried it. Yes, dill. Yes, cabbage. Yes, yes, yes. Then the meat. It had a sweet flavor. Venison? No, not that strong. It tasted oddly like the simple borsch our Olga made for her family.

My cousin smiled across the table at her smiling husband. "We have hired Baron Tretyakov's old cook. He replaced her with a man from Moscow."

"Imagine," said Mama, "a *man* in the baron's kitchen."

"That's how it's done in Moscow," said Anna, always an echo of Avram when it came to the ins and outs of grand society. "How do you like it, Libby?" And then to the others. "How do you like it, my dears?"

"It's delicious," said Jake, hardly looking up from his plate.

"I like it, thank you." Rachel gave her hostess her best company smile.

"Me too," said Nessa.

And me. "I've only had something this good a few times in my life."

Sarah said, "I like Olga's soup."

"Olga didn't make this soup, little one," said Anna.

"But it tastes like it. She puts pork meat in her soup, too."

"What's that she said?" demanded Avram.

All the spoons of all the Vorontsovs stopped. Sarah sank into her high-backed chair.

I fished around in my bowl, speared a piece of meat, and held it, dripping, for all to see. "I think she's right."

"Pass it here," thundered Avram.

I sent it to Rachel, who sent it to Papa, who held it at

arm's length and made a sniffing sound, then passed it to Avram. A pink borsch dribble on the white tablecloth marked the route of the unlucky chunk.

I once saw a jeweler examine a ruby with a loup — I always wondered what he was looking for. That was the way Avram, breathing loudly in the silence, his ruddy complexion redder than ever, looked at the meat.

"Pork." Cousin Avram was a man of the world — he might not know pork when he saw it, but he knew when to accede to an expert. With the fire in his eyes he usually reserved for a bank employee who added 20 and 20 and got 50, he summoned the new cook, the baron's excook, to the table.

"Your honor," she said to him, tears falling onto her wringing hands, "how was I to know?" From somewhere in the folds of the apron that covered her wide body, she produced a blue babushka and wiped her eyes and then the little drops of sweat on her forehead. "I am hired by a prominent family with a good Russian name. How was I to know?" Then, as if the sun had just broken through on an overcast day, her broad face lit up in a gap-toothed smile. "Your honor, we can call Father Arseny to bless the pork — then surely it will be all right."

We all laughed, Avram the loudest.

The soup went out the window, but the baron's excook stayed. Because really, the best possible event had occurred — the Vorontsovs had passed as Russian. Truly, how *was* she to know?

11

——◇—◇—◇——

Just a month after our dinner at the Vorontsovs, some events occurred that would alter our daily lives for a while, and eventually forever.

I had a bad dream: the family was loading a ship-sized balagole to begin a journey to America. I was walking in circles with a slow, old, buff-colored horse, hitched up to my father's felt-making machine. The wool smelled like ammonia and dirt mixed together. In a far corner of the room, some peasants held a squirming sheep, which bleated and bleated because a knife was at its throat. One of the moujiks kept yelling to me, "faster, faster," but I couldn't. I called for my family. They went on piling into the wagon, which had just grown a sail. "I'm coming," Cousin Avram said. He loaded his bank safe into the balagole. "Anna is staying. She just got a new dress from Paris and she won't leave it alone." Everyone nodded. "Don't go without me," I yelled. They turned their backs and climbed into the boat-wagon. I pulled at my harness; the horse started to run. I couldn't keep up. The wagon plunged off.

I jerked awake and kicked Sarah, who didn't move. Oh, that wonderful feeling that steals into your mind when a bad dream lets go. You aren't being chased off a cliff. Your family isn't leaving for America without you.

I turned over and fell into a peaceful sleep.

I woke late to the ringing of church bells, but it wasn't Sunday. They rang and rang. Jake and I hurried to town just in time to see a big sleigh drawn by four horses pull up to the market square. On the back of the sleigh was a huge picture of Tsar Nicholas. Two men in heavy fur coats and hats — one looking enough like the Tsar to be his brother, the other a slant-eyed Tatar — jumped out and read a proclamation. The Japanese had snuck up on the Russian ships in Port Arthur, China. It was war. Every city and village must get ready.

The church bells rang all day. People ran through the streets and gathered in little groups. "Did you hear? Pavel is going to enlist." "They're calling up fourteen-year-old boys." "The police chief says we've already drubbed those yellow monkeys." The rumors ran faster than the boots that carried them, and for the next few days we were caught up in war fever.

Even when I'm as old as Grandma Vorontsov, February 13, 1904, the fourth day after the Tsar's proclamation, will remain clear in my mind. It was one of those bitter days when hats were pulled down and collars turned up, and you knew each person was thinking only of a hot glass of tea and dinner in the oven, and not at all about the war. I watched and listened as Klym Sereda stood alone in the yellow glow of the window of the kerosene store, drunk already in the late afternoon, talking to anyone who passed by, but no one paid attention.

"I'd join first thing. I'd show those slant-eyed bastards how a white man fights." He smacked the bottom of a bottle on the palm of his hand and the cork shot out. "If the baron didn't need me, I'd be off tomorrow." A swig of vodka. "I would have been on the train. But that Shchastiyvliy, he won't let anyone else touch him."

By the time I got home it was dark and everyone was in the kitchen trying to comfort a sobbing Natalka, her pale, yellow face splotched with red, her long, skinny body twitching with each sob. Her boyfriend, Afanasy, had left on the troop train in the morning. Now, even if he came home on leave there would be no wedding, as it was an unwritten law among the peasants that a soldier couldn't marry a young girl.

In my drawer was a tiny icon of Saint Olga given me by Marusya. I ran upstairs to get it. As I rifled through the underwear, socks, and hairpins, I came across the burned piece of paper, the poem, that the Serbs had dropped. Once again I read it through:

> Heart hungry, I never crossed
> Your threshold with a grief
> That was not mine.

Maybe they meant they always carried the sadness of exiles with them. I couldn't really understand it.

I found the icon and ran back downstairs to the kitchen.

"Look, Natalka. I found this in the snow. It's Saint Olga. Isn't she the saint of lovers separated? Maybe I was meant to find her and give her to you. It means Afanasy will serve his enlistment safe and sound. He'll come back to marry you."

How gratefully they looked at me when Natalka, her lips pressed to the icon, sank to her knees, crossed herself, and rose smiling. Only Sarah looked at me strangely. I think she must have known I was harboring a saint in my bloomers.

Then the house settled into its routine. Before dinner Papa sat at the kitchen table with a pile of newspapers, his lips moving, his finger recording his place. Nessa and Rachel set a table for their dolls in a corner of the dining room, cutting pieces of paper into tiny bowls of "Olga's borsch" and platters of "kulebiaka." Jake reread his magazine article about cattle ranching in America, while Sarah's dark head bent over her animal picture book. Grandma and Mama knelt on the floor, pencils in hand, studying a large linen cloth.

I was feeling restless and walked from room to room, looking out each window at the snow falling into drifts — one of the heaviest snowfalls in years people had been saying lately. This certainly was a year to remember. The murder, the fire in Davidov's bakery, Papa in jail, the gypsies, now the war with Japan. I thought about Klym Sereda, his hat turning white in the snow, bragging about "thumping the Japs." I thought about Afanasy, who hated the cold, going off to war, and the government having a terrible time providing woolen uniforms. Though the kitchen was soup-pot warm, I shivered. My breath made a soft cloud on the windowpane.

After dinner, we lingered at the table, blinking sleepily at the candlelight. The girls were carried off to bed, the lamps turned down. Inside our big white house, darkness and silence lay over us.

Twice that night, I woke up. I thought I heard a man singing outside the factory. The voice merged with my dream of marching soldiers. The second time a smell woke me — a peasant's fire, clearing a field in autumn. My window glowed, but it was still night. Outside, our factory was burning in the steady fall of snow.

"Sarah! Sarah, wake up!" I shook her hard; I brought her face close to mine.

"Sweetheart, there's a fire outside. I want you to go to the front path and stand by the well. So you won't get hurt. Go there and wait for us. Take the comforter. Okay?" I left her reaching for a shoe.

The hall was foggy with smoke. My father was just opening his door.

"It's the factory, Papa. It must be in the house now too."

"The children!" my mother cried.

"You two get everyone out." Papa ran toward the stairs.

"I already sent Sarah out," I yelled to my mother as she ran to Nessa and Rachel's room.

I looked back into my room, thick now with smoke. "Sarah, are you there?" No one answered.

Grandma, her hair plaited for bedtime, clutching a

package to her breast, pushed open her door and called, "Everyone follow me."

We found Natalka sobbing in a corner and we all got out just before the house lit up into a single fire. We stood shivering by the well, under the bare linden trees, in the deep snow, Papa in his white nightcap, looking at each of us, quickly, as though counting us up. I followed his eyes. Then he disappeared into the front door, dark with smoke.

We waited, a family of snow people, frozen, white, watching the orange and blue feathers of the fire until Papa emerged with Sarah in his arms — Sarah who always wakes up twice. In her hand she clutched a crumpled brown shoe.

He laid her on the ground and rubbed her face with snow. Her eyes flickered, then opened, amazed at the circle of family faces staring down at her. "Why are we outside?" she asked.

Jake and Papa ran to the barn to let the horses out. Then the factory roof collapsed in on itself and the flames inside reached for the sky. Then the hotel, then the house — our home.

My father looked so puzzled, not sad, not angry or worried, but as if some question were posing itself deep inside him.

"Where will we go?" asked my brother.

My father looked at him but did not answer.

We heard sleigh bells. It was Nikon and the oradnick. They motioned to us. We crowded into the sleigh and hurtled off into the night. In the minutes it took to get across town to the Troyans, I must have fallen asleep, or just stopped thinking and seeing.

Our fingers and minds numbed with cold and shock, we stood in front of the great oven in the Troyans' kitchen, waiting for the heat to bring us back to life, just as months ago Count Dusan and his troupe had done in *our* kitchen, in front of *our* oven.

"We'll hide you. Hide you. All of you," said the oradnick, his voice a high-pitched whisper. "In the morning the peasants might do something. They think well of you, but you never know. There's the war."

His words ratta-tatted out in little drumbeats. At first I didn't understand what he meant. Then I remembered the bakery fire. The peasants might say we burned the factory to collect the insurance. It had happened before.

The oradnick and my father sat in the kitchen, talking softly, while we got tucked away in strange beds, in a house that was not ours.

12

One of the first things you notice about living in someone else's house is that it smells wrong. Our kitchen had a sweet, oniony smell, while the Troyans' smelled less of food and more of carbolic soap. Marusya's room, which we shared, had a faint odor of musk oil that came from the rainbow bottles on her dressing table; my room had smelled of fresh sheets and sunshine.

We were forced to hide at the Troyans until first the police and then a representative of the peasants' council found whether Papa had set the fire. The peasant, a prosperous tobacco farmer who helped decide Lev Davidov's innocence, knew and respected my father, so we were hopeful.

The day after the fire the oradnick paid a quiet visit to Cousin Avram and arranged for clothes to be delivered to us. As a converted Jew, he couldn't be too open about helping us; the superstitious peasants might think all that holy water and incense hadn't done the job.

The Troyans' house was bigger than ours, though not as grand as the Vorontsovs'. There was a big spare bedroom where Mama and Papa slept with the three little girls, and of course Jake shared Nikon's plain, orderly room. Mrs. Troyan, the youngest daughter of a minor nobleman, embroidered in a sewing room as perfectly appointed as a satin pincushion, while Mr. Troyan's book-lined study, with its leather chairs and spinning globe, was used by us children for our favorite game. One of us would close our eyes and spin the globe. When it was about to stop the others would yell, "Now," and the blind person would put his finger on the map and in twenty questions have to tell where it had landed. When it was Jake's turn he always guessed America first. In a corner of the study stood a tall clock that didn't work, its motionless face painted with a deep star-filled sky of midnight blue. If you looked closely you could see each star was a child's face.

It was strange, fitting the Kagans in with the Troyans. Over those weeks I never felt like myself. They were so kind, but it was as though their family were the grown-ups and ours the children. We didn't know how the household worked: what time they ate, where to put the dirty clothes, or if you had to tiptoe around their father. But we learned.

My mother insisted that we all pitch in around the house. I helped their old cook, Marfa, prepare meals — Marfa who shuffled around the kitchen in felt slippers, her holey stockings rolled down around her ankles, a cigarette hanging from the corner of her mouth. She had come with Mrs. Troyan as part of the marriage dowry and though her varenky were rubbery and her blini stamped with burn marks as if a little black doily had been pressed into each one, she was good-hearted and never complained about having to feed eight extra people.

Jake took care of little things around the Troyans' house, sharpening all the knives, putting new wicks in the lamps, replacing several of the rickety attic steps. As he worked, he sang Ukrainian peasant songs, switching occasionally to the American tune, *Yankee Doodle*, that the oradnick taught him. Once he disappeared for half a day. That night he called us into Mr. Troyan's study to see the pendulum on the tall star-faced clock swinging in perfect time.

Mama decided that the house-children should help me in the kitchen, but they had developed a crush on Marusya and managed to avoid kitchen work by perpetually fetching my friend's hairbrush or her dancing shoes. It turned out that Marusya had always longed for younger sisters. I was delighted to lend her two of mine. She got out her old dolls and played house with them, and every afternoon at four, when she wasn't at dance class, she held a class of her own for Nessa and Rachel. Outfitted in my friend's old ballet shoes, they spent half their stay at the Troyans somewhere between first and fifth positions.

Sarah had no job except to be quiet and stay out of everyone's way. She found dark, secret places to hide — the space under the cellar stairs, the old laundry chute from the big spare bedroom to the pantry, which she never fell down because she was too cautious to even poke her head into the upstairs part of it. Once, in the attic, I came across her sitting quietly, watching a few gray, long-tailed field mice eat some grains of kasha just a few inches from her hand. "They come in in winter," she explained, "to see me, their queen."

Mrs. Troyan, whose skin was the color of milk with the cream skimmed off, ran her household from the morning room sofa, a box of bonbons by her side. She was plump and chatty; every move she made tinkled with bracelets. She wouldn't hear of Mama's helping around the house, so our mother had to sit with her and embroider and drink great quantities of sweet tea. Maybe that's why Mama was so sharp with us during that time. Grandma, however, refused to give in to our hostess. Grandma cleaned. The Troyans had plenty of servants, and Grandma had never been a great one for cleaning, but something possessed her. Just about any hour of the day she could be seen, her head wrapped in a white babushka, dust rag or mop in hand, on her knees or on a stool, rubbing, rubbing. When I asked her why she did it, she answered, "Because I need to."

Living in the same house with Nikon was confusing. For the first time in my life my appetite deserted me. When I felt him watching across the table, my stomach would turn over and lose interest in the forkful of golden-brown potato kugel I was about to send down to it. It would play the same trick on me when I met him by surprise on the stairs, or when he came in the kitchen to watch me cook.

We talked a lot in the evenings when he came home from the gymnasium, where he was the first student in the school in mathematics and science. One night, after dinner, while Marusya was reading to my sisters (she had hinted once or twice that her brother was taking up a lot of my time), he and I climbed to the attic to look for the set of dolls he had won in a speed skating race when he was just five. He had been the only boy entered under the age of ten, so they put him with the girls and he won. In the same dark, spider-web corner where I found Queen Sarah feeding kasha to her field-mice subjects, we found them, a set of roly-poly wooden girl-dolls with yellow braids, who fit, perfectly, one inside the other.

Brushing away the cobwebs, he made a seat for us out of some dusty green-velvet curtains. We leaned against the rough planks of the wall and I listened as he told me of his life's ambition — to be a doctor and help the people in the villages who had no decent medical care. I recited the story of my dead uncles and the felsher who said, "Don't give them any water." His eyes grew angry; he brushed back the lock of hair from his forehead. "Yes, that's just the kind of thing we must keep from happening," he said. "Everyone — not just rich people — deserves to see a real doctor." He has his whole life planned out — how long he'll be in school, when he will get married. He wants to start a hospital in Dmitrovka where the peasants can come from all over and pay only what they can afford. I watched him, his eyes shining, his straight brows touching as he frowned in concentration, lost in his dream of the future. He had told no one else of his plans. "I don't want to talk about it; I just want to do it," he said. "But I wanted to tell *you*." Then he kissed me — my first kiss — cool and smelling of bay soap and pencils, but not as thrilling as I expected. What really excited me were his plans to do good in the world — and that I was the only person who knew about them.

Nikon idolized his father, the oradnick. "He knows so much, and he never even went to university." The studious absent-minded mayor got along well with *my* father. Samuel Troyan and Papa spent hours in the study where they pored over the huge collection of books on the American Revolution. At dinner they discussed Thomas Jefferson and Thomas Paine, Benjamin Franklin and Marshall Lafayette — all strangers to me. They talked philosophy and politics, agreeing that the ordinary man should have a say in his government and that many of the Tsar's laws were unfair — especially to the Jews.

The oradnick, a pencil stuck in his curly hair, his spectacles halfway down his nose, would clear his throat. "Huh. That's one of the reasons I converted. Didn't like the odds. The odds." He had a habit of picking up his wine glass and staring into it as if life were fairer seen through red wine from the mountain slopes of the Crimea. "My father was a poor tailor from Cernigov. He used to say God never did anything for him and he was only too happy to return the favor.

"I love to read. I wanted to be a professor in a great university. When I was twelve I was apprenticed to a shoemaker. At sixteen I went to work for a gentile who made boots for the army. I was a salesman, and to my surprise I had a knack for it." He still seemed surprised. "Before the gentile took me into the business, he asked if

101

I'd convert. 'Better for business,' he said. I did. I did. Two years later, a stroke. He died. It was *my* business. I was twenty-two. I married Lisabeta. Sold my business for a lot of money. Now I read books. And help run Dmitrovka. I am what I am. It's all the same to me."

Every day the three little girls would ask Mama how long we had to stay there. She said, "I'll tell you when I know." At last the authorities made their judgment: "Arson — guilty party unknown." Now we could come out of hiding, though we had no place to go — except for Papa, who had to go to jail for ten days.

Mr. Troyan went to the police station to see if he could lighten my father's sentence. Ten days was a long time, especially for a man who *didn't* start a fire. We all crowded into the sunny morning room. When he returned he squinted at Papa over the top of his glasses.

"What did you ever do to Tropinin?"

"Nothing."

"Hmm. I just met some of your friends leaving the jail. They tried to buy you out of the sentence. They said he kept talking about a cousin in Konotop. Then he threw them out. Because you 'sent' them to bribe an officer of the Tsar, he was going to change your sentence. To six months."

The room was quiet. Through the open door to the study, I could hear the ticking of the tall clock.

"But we worked something out. An accommodation." Then, as if it had been blown out by a sudden wind, the habitual kindness of his expression was replaced by cold

102

anger. "He needs to know that he can't play with the law in Dmitrovka.

"I told him, 'As my father-in-law Nobleman Sazonov says, "When the sun is shining, don't go fishing for trouble." For trouble. Things run smoothly here. We look good to the authorities in Cernigov. Those who have the need, take what extras come their way.'

"Tropinin stared at his boots. I told him, 'Abraham Kagan is too well liked. You jail him for six months, the Jews are unhappy. The peasants who bring their wool to him are unhappy. No. Everybody should be happy. My noble father-in-law says, "If you muddy up the pond, you can't see the treasure chest resting on the bottom." '

"I suggested he could find a poor moujik to sleep in his nice warm jail. For ten nights. The man is hasty. But greed runs him.

"Come here, little sister." He pulled Sarah onto his lap. She looked into his face, then snuggled against him. "Your sentence starts tomorrow. Tomorrow. Jail in the daytime. Home with your family at night. Not so bad. Ten days."

Events happened fast after that. Papa went to jail. We found a house. And so, two weeks and three days after they took us in, we left the Troyans for a two-room thatched cottage near our old house on the other side of town.

13

♦—♦—♦

It was my Great-great-aunt Libby's dress that helped me change my mind about America. Every day we were at the Troyans Jake had pestered me. "It's the only place. We can be whatever we want there." But I didn't know. I loved Dmitrovka. It was my home.

The new house was near our old one, on the road to town, closer in. It had two rooms with dirt floors. In the front room was the large brick stove, which served for cooking, baking, heating, and sleeping. As in our old house, there was a bench all around it with hollow places to dry clothes and ledges for sleeping and sitting. We stoked it with slow-burning birch logs that kept the house cozy all day and night. The only piece of furniture was an old blue-painted table with one leg shorter than the others. It was so small it made us seem like a family of twelve instead of eight. Our friends donated the eight unrelated chairs that, try as we might, wouldn't fit around the table at the same time. Mama took to feeding us at two shifts.

"The family will be all right here," Grandma proclaimed, looking as satisfied as a general who had found a secure bivouac for his troops. The roof was newly thatched and the house had been well cared for, but germs don't walk up and shake your hand, so my mother declared war and we swept and scrubbed and whitewashed all day. By the time we finished, there wasn't a germ left alive to tell war stories. The dirt floors were tamped down, and the walls inside shone white as the snow that lay in the fields around the house. We brought in fresh straw pallets to sleep on, but the best bed, the platform of the oven, was only big enough for four, so we took turns.

How quickly a house becomes familiar. This one was small and there were so few things in it to make a life, and not much privacy, so as the evenings went on we would move our chairs further away from the table, separating ourselves as best we could.

It was odd how we each gravitated toward certain chairs, reclaiming them every day as if our names were painted on the backs. With its slats jointed like the graceful horsetails that grew near the pond, mine had once been beautiful. Papa took the high ladder-back with the rush seat, Mama, the frayed pink-satin boudoir chair, while Grandma commandeered the captain's chair, its arms splayed and determined. Sarah was left with the one no one wanted, a home-made wobbly affair with a seat that slanted to the left and a back so nicked it resembled one of mother's embroidery patterns. And if that

105

weren't enough, it was so big it swallowed her up. We all offered to trade with her, but she wouldn't hear of it. "I like this one — I can play boat in it. And read. It's good." She smoothed the worn seat with her finger.

After school I was in charge of Sarah, which was like taking care of the air — it's quiet and always there. But one day when I came out of the back room she *wasn't* there. I opened the door and called. Then I saw her footprints in the snow. Like little snowshoe rabbit tracks, they led toward the woods that started about a quarter of a mile behind the cottage. I saw her long before I got there, the winter sun shining on her red coat and dark hair, squatting motionless at the edge of the birch forest. The air, the trees, everything was motionless as the inside of a mirror; I moved toward her carefully, not wanting to shatter the stillness. Then Sarah spoke to someone, her small voice chipping at the silence. A pair of red foxes, their tails drooping, their black ears cocked, listened. "Now, *you*, the big one, you take care of the baby. Brush her hair and carry her out of the house if it catches fire. You, little sister, try to talk more, play with the other foxes instead of being by yourself. They'll like you better. And always, always, sleep with someone else. If you sleep alone, you could burn up. Your queen has spoken."

As Sarah stood, the foxes turned slowly, deliberately, and trotted off into the woods. She came toward me as serenely as if I had found her reading under the peach tree in the orchard. She took my hand and we started back to the house.

It's odd. Sometimes people don't talk about what most

disturbs them. Sarah could tell the foxes what she couldn't tell any person — even me. Papa is the same way. All the days he spent in the jail he never said a word about it at home. He went off every morning, his hat brushed, his lunch in a wicker basket, as if he were going to the factory. Maybe he told Mama about it, but if so none of us children ever knew.

The fourth day in the new house, while Papa was still in jail, Grandma called us together.

"I have something to show you. Something even I've never seen."

She produced a brown-paper parcel, the one she had carried from the house the night of the fire, and set it on the kitchen table. The paper, crumpled and yellow, was tied with frayed hemp.

I settled into Sarah's big chair and took her on my lap as Grandma, pressing at her cheeks, began:

"It belonged to your Great-great-aunt Libby, who our Libby is named for. It hasn't been opened in eighty years.

"My Aunt Libby, my mother's sister, was a very beautiful girl — her eyes were the color of wild lupin. And of course she sang like one of God's own angels. No one in that family could even carry a tune, and she used to tease her parents that the gypsies taught her. They wanted to send her away to study with a great teacher, but it was an expensive proposition, too expensive for a family with nine children. Then their prayers were answered. A powerful nobleman heard her sing and promised to pay for her musical education. He wanted to show off his protegée and made arrangements for her to sing for him and his guests at a grand party. My mother stayed up all night making her sister a beautiful dress to wear. The day she finished it, a gentile boy was found murdered behind the synagogue and the Jews were blamed. A pogrom was in the air. The family packed what they could and fled. On their journey Libby came down with influenza. She died on the very night she was to have sung for the nobleman. Fourteen years old.

"My mother wrapped up the dress forever. But now our Libby could use it."

Grandma opened the package. A sheer white cloth, a dress, emerged from the tissue and she gave it a gentle shake the way you do to get rid of wrinkles. Then, it was a dress no more — with a faint tearing sound the old threads gave way into strips of lacy cloth that resembled the bandages the women cut for the soldiers fighting in China. Everyone sighed. On my lap Sarah was still as a field mouse.

I rubbed a piece of the hem between my fingers, as Nessa and Rachel began to sniffle. I could feel something hard under the cloth; without thinking I ripped it open. A coin clattered to the table.

Grandma grabbed for it. She placed it in the flattened palm of her hand and examined it carefully, then explained how the Jews, when they had to leave town in a hurry, would sew jewels or money into their clothing.

"So now, my granddaughter, you have been given a gift from your namesake. An inheritance. From Libby to Libby."

The gold coin glittered as she handed it across the table. The lettering was scrolly and foreign. "Arabic," offered Grandma, pointing to a lion, the rayed sun behind him, flourishing a curved sword in his paw. I held it tightly. Fourteen. I would be fourteen in just a few weeks.

Later that night as I lay on the ledge of the stove, the coin in the pocket of my nightgown, Sarah squeezed in next to me. "Libby, when we go to America are you going to sew the coin in your dress?"

"Who says we're going to America? Go to sleep."

I turned over and the coin poked my chest, the coin I got because my ancestors had to come away from their home in haste. Jews being chased from their homes. It had gone on since the Bible, when the kingdom of Judah was conquered and thousands of people were sent to Babylonia. Our situation, of course, was different. We were forced out by the accident of a fire, and certainly if we had to leave Dmitrovka in haste there would be no worry about what to take since we had nothing, except for my inheritance. I felt lucky to have inherited the coin from Aunt Libby, but I didn't want to inherit her life. She didn't get to be a famous singer because of a pogrom. What wouldn't I get to be if we stayed in Dmitrovka? And Jake? And what if my father lost another business to fire? Without insurance we would have nothing again. We had to leave Dmitrovka, to go to America. I didn't want to, but we had to.

I climbed down from the stove and made my way in the dark, around the sleeping bodies, to my brother. I knelt and whispered in his ear, "I've changed my mind. We have to go to America."

He opened his eyes wide and said, "Look out for the bonbon," then he turned his back and rolled into a ball.

When I told him the next morning, he laughed and hugged me. "Look out for the bonbon. It'll land on you before you can leave for America."

Luckily for us our cellar had escaped the fire, so we had plenty to eat. The first Friday after my father got out of jail, Mama made a special dinner — pot roast with eggplant and the white mushrooms we had picked last June from under the cherry trees.

"The roast is delicious. My mama's such a good cook." Jake stood up and bowed toward mother.

Papa lifted his glass of wine. "To Bayla — a good cook, a good mother, a good woman." Then he smiled at her the way he smiled at Mr. Polishuk, who bought wool from him. "So, my dear, now that you're looking at Dmitrovka from two rooms with dirt floors, does it still look as good?"

His question cut off the conversation like a scythe through winter wheat. Mama stared at her plate, and we all stared at Mama.

"It was different before the fire. The house. The factory. Such a good life. But America. At Ellis Island they humiliate you. And we would be starting all over." She shrugged. "But now, we're starting over anyway. So . . . it might as well be in a new country." She almost whispered it.

Papa's face was expressionless, as though he wouldn't

commit himself to joy until she made a commitment to America.

"I'm ready," she said. Her face was flushed; she looked young.

Grandma Vorontsov gave me a triumphant smile.

Sarah got up and stood between Jake and me.

"We're going on a big boat to America," I said into her curly hair. "How do you like that?"

"It depends. If it's a very big boat, I like it. If it's a little one, I don't."

The questions flew at my father.

"How much will it cost?" "How will we be able to talk to anybody?"

Papa explained that first we would need permits from the government, then visas from the Americans. He was worried about Jake — they sometimes were reluctant to give permits to boys who were close to military age. According to Papa, the authorities would love to see all the Jews leave except for a few bankers like Avram, to mind their money, and people like Baron Gunzberg, to build their railroads, yet when a Jew gets up the nerve to go, they pretend to need him.

As for the language, we could learn English in school, just as soon as we got there. The real problem was money. Our savings were almost gone and Papa had no job.

We concocted projects: Papa could start a business like his old one. The customers would all come back; Jake would help. Or he could make fur coats and rugs — he could do wonders with animal skins. Rachel suggested that some rich relative might be good enough to die and leave us all his money; while I preferred Cousin Avram alive, I wouldn't miss anyone on the Kagan side. Too bad there was no money there. Mama's knitting needles click-clacked as we schemed. She was making a plum-colored scarf for Rachel. We all needed warm things, but Rachel's mourning for her beautiful burned clothes was so loud and so deep that mother put that scarf ahead of everything else.

There was a knock on the door, and in a flurry of snow and cloudy breath, Avram and Anna blew into the hut, filling it with their dark, glossy furs, and their scents — cigars and violets. The Vorontsovs had brought clothes for everyone, a set of dishes, a big metal cook pot, and a wooden stand for Papa to hang his pants on. (Avram said no gentleman should be without one.) If the room was crowded before, now we were like dough in a bread pan, warm, rising, and threatening to push over.

Cousin Avram lit a cigar, puffing until the stubby end glowed. "Abraham," he said. "Anna had an idea — and it's a good one. I hope you'll like it . . . I want you to come and work for me in the bank." He watched Papa through a puff of smoke, knowing the fierceness of my father's pride, for the job was at the bottom of the ladder, though each rung was a golden one.

Papa walked around the table and stretched out his hand. "My friend, you could not offer me anything that I want or need more than an honest job. But I must tell you that just tonight we have made a decision — to go to

112

America as soon as we get the money. So if you want me until then, I will come."

"Well . . . that's not exactly what I had in mind. I need someone I can trust. I'm gone so much. America." Then he threw up his hands and smiled. "I'll be glad to have you."

And so it was settled. Papa would work for Cousin Avram until he had saved enough to buy the passage to America.

Suddenly it didn't matter about sleeping on the floor. It didn't matter that we tripped over each other in our tiny house, bumping heads and elbows all day long. We were going to America!

Gently, insistently, Cousin Anna tapped her husband's shoulder. "You *are* going to tell, aren't you?"

Avram suddenly looked like a man whose suit was too small for him. The greeny glow of the cheap oil lamp pinched the roundness from his face.

"You must tell."

"All right! I've been hearing some rumors. But I don't want you to go off and do anything crazy." He stopped as though waiting for a question.

"The baron's foreman, the one who drinks too much, has been bragging that he set your fire." Cousin Avram said it matter-of-factly, the way you'd tell your mother what you did at school that day. "Whether this is true or not, remember the baron thinks Sereda's uncanny with horses. He feels lucky to have him. So I don't know what to say." He sent me a warning look, then glanced from

113

Papa to Cousin Anna and around the room to the rest
as though he didn't want to look at anybody long enough
for them to question him.

Cousin Anna spoke up. "Avram wasn't going to say
anything. I told him to. If it were me, I'd want to hear."

Avram made ready to go. Three sentences of inde-
pendence were all she was allowed.

"We don't want to stir a pot that doesn't need stirring,"
he warned.

When they were gone, Jake was the first to speak. "I
knew it. Didn't I tell you, Lib?"

He had and I told him it was wishful thinking, that it
was easy to blame one person for all the bad things in
Dmitrovka. "We'll get him. We'll — "

"Children!" Papa's tone withered our words, but not
our outrage. "Starting from today, we Kagans are no
longer citizens of Dmitrovka. America must always be in
our thoughts. We cannot afford to do anything that will
jeopardize our leaving. We must tiptoe around. If we are
noticed, we must smile politely. The waves on the ocean
we can't control, but we can tread the waters of Dmitrovka
carefully . . . carefully."

Papa was right; the future in America was more important than the present. But people shouldn't be allowed
to get away with wrongdoing. It just encouraged them
to go out and do more harm. Klym Sereda killed a man
and got away with it. He set our fire and was going to get
away with that. The next thing he did would be partly
our fault, too.

14

◇◇◇

"So, Samuel Troyan got your visas. A good man. He doesn't look it, but he knows which strings to pull and how hard to pull them," said Cousin Avram.

It was a glittery late March day, half winter, half spring, and Jake and I were flying along with Avram in his troika. The brass bells on the horses' bridles rang through the clear air. Last night's snowflakes had frozen in their separate shapes, scattering a winter garden of crystal sweet williams, violets, and forget-me-nots.

The sky was a thick blue. The birches, their pale etched trunks casting long shadows on the snow, stood at attention as we flew by, like the poor Russian soldiers being reviewed by the generals in far-off South China.

In a small clearing a group of peasants warmed their hands around a fire. It wasn't until we passed them that I saw the animal cage and wondered if they might be gypsies. But I was too excited to care. Avram had borrowed me again.

The baron was having a skating party for Tatiana on the pond where last summer the rowboats had floated. As we drove along, our cousin recited his newest business dealings with the baron, a loan on a house in Kiev and some timberland north of Dmitrovka. And if the baron didn't spend less time giving parties and more time tending to his affairs, the bank would end up with a townhouse and a lot of trees. The baron was surely going to have to put Tatiana and his title out on the marriage market to fish for a rich husband. "And she's a plain little thing, though the title's fancy enough."

Coming from the peasant hut with dirt floors, how we savored the thought of the luxury of that day. Not that we didn't have money. Papa was adept at banking, and Avram was delighted and gave him weekly raises in the hope he would decide to stay. But the money that would have gone for a larger house and new clothes was put away every week in a black tin box in the big bank safe.

We drove by the beet fields that in the summer had swarmed with workers. Now they were quiet under a sugary crust of snow. The bare limbs of the cherry trees were lined in frost, and as the horses turned up the lane to the mansion, I remembered climbing *our* trees, the smoothness of the fruit in my hand, the juice filling my mouth.

"Haaaaaaaalt. Stop." Klym Sereda staggered into the middle of the road, his gloveless hands pushing a stop signal in the air. Up ahead, red ribbons flapped in the wind; another troika was bringing guests to the skating party.

We slowed to avoid running him down.

"Whateryoudoinghere? You people aren't wanted here." He stamped his feet like a child in a tantrum.

With a crack of the whip, Avram left the overseer staring at the marks of our runners on the snow.

"I can't believe the baron keeps him on," said Jake. Cousin Avram didn't answer — he only puffed his cheeks and pushed out two short breaths.

"Avram, *please*. Now that the baron owes you money, he'll listen, and he'll be grateful. He'll give you the rest of his banking business."

He chuckled, as if he'd been told a mildly funny joke. "I might do it. But . . . well, you'll understand when you grow up."

I already understood that when a grown-up tells you that it means one of two things: he doesn't want to take the time to explain something, or he doesn't want you to know what he's really thinking.

Then I was being handed down into the laughter and brightness of Tatiana's party. Tables were set outside as they had been in summer, their snowy cloths resembling the broad lawns and empty flower beds of the estate. People helped themselves at the steaming silver samovars of tea, the platters of dumplings, spiced honey cake, doughnut puffs, and almond horns, while peasant women in red-fringed scarves offered around baskets of sticky buns. A shabby peacock mingled on the terrace, pecking at the pots of red geraniums, strutting behind a babushkaed servant like a naughty, mimicking child.

Out on the lawn the baron had made an ice hill. The

117

children, and grown-ups too, climbed the wooden stairs and sledded down the frozen surface, hollering and laughing. The terrace, the lawn, and the people all glittered in a way that couldn't happen in summer; the snow-reflected early spring light made every object separate and bright.

Cousin Avram deposited us at the skating pond and went off to join the circle of men in sable coats laughing together on the terrace that overlooked the pond.

At the wooden benches by the edge of the ice, Jake and I warmed our hands at one of the bonfires burning in iron tubs.

"Lib, you're terrific. If I talked to Avram like that, he would've made me turn in my skates and go home."

"He likes me. He hears what I say." I pulled on one of the new skates our cousin had given us for the occasion and stomped my foot into it. "Maybe it's because he doesn't get along with his own children. He knew he was wrong — I could see it in his eyes. He's bargaining with himself. Maybe his good side will win."

I watched the skaters make their way around the pond. A tall man bent low to his companion, a boy of about four, who sucked his thumb right through his mitten as the pair skated stiffly through the throng. Three girls in identical blue outfits held hands and giggled as they glided past an old lady in black who skated backwards.

A spray of ice and the flash of a red skirt. "Hello, you two. Hurry up. You're missing it all." As the four of us took the ice, I began to tell the Troyans what happened with Sereda. Marusya said of course Cousin Avram would talk to the baron now. I so wanted to believe her.

118

The organ-grinder from last summer, in a new bottle green jacket, skated through the crowd carrying his monkey in front of him. The red-eyed animal held a silver tray containing a cut crystal glass of wine. As he sailed across the ice he turned his head from side to side, looking, looking. For just a second, my eyes caught his old, sad ones.

How could Avram, who was rich and respected, let Sereda, a glorified hired man, talk to him like that and refuse to do anything about it? There he was, on the terrace with the baron, their heads close together — maybe he was telling him. They stepped off the terrace and out across the lawn. I had to hear what they were saying. We took off our skates and sneaked off through the cherry orchard down the edge of a snowpacked path that led somewhere into the unfamiliar territory of the Tretyakov estate, eavesdropping on the baron and Cousin Avram.

The deep snow that muffled our footsteps slowed us. Luckily the two men strolled unhurriedly down the path, stopping occasionally as their talk dictated. Hidden in the forest of thick gray trunks we caught only snatches of words.

"My wife . . . living well, Vorontsov . . . on me to see that she continues to do so . . . who do I . . . I count on you."

We picked our way carefully, avoiding fallen branches and the hip-high drifts.

"I'm glad, Your Excellency." Avram's voice managed to sound both respectful and confident. ". . . my pleasure . . . a family who lives so graciously . . . who keeps to the old traditions." They walked on past an open shelter with a

119

tin roof that shone in the early afternoon sun. It was stacked to the top with wagon wheels. ". . . a good idea to increase your wheat. . . . The war . . . prices high."

". . . Sereda says the peasants are lazy. Grisha. Zachar . . . worked so well for us . . . slackers now. Thank God for Sereda. I have no head for farming. You haven't seen my horse. Shchastiyvliy . . . race . . . in June at the Derby in Moscow."

Another shed, this one walled, shut off the talk. We scrambled around it.

". . . you'll want to bet your bank on him. Come and have a look."

They picked up their pace, skirting the ice and mud in the road. A peasant with a stovepipe hat and two medals on his long, black coat walked by leading a horse. When he saw the baron he pulled the animal off to the side and waited till the men passed.

"Cousin Avram has all the guts of a dead chicken," hissed Jake.

"And the baron's got the brains of one," I countered. "Sure Klym Sereda knows how to manage this place." I was angry, not so much at Avram, but at myself for keeping alive the hope that he would do the right thing. I should have known. "Business pulls the cart; money greases the wheels."

Since there was no hope for Avram, we decided to salvage something from our walk by seeing the wondrous Shchastiyvliy, so we made our way through the orchard, coming out between a storehouse and the stone building where the blacksmith worked. The smith, a stocky blond man with eyebrows that made a bushy mustache across his forehead, had his forge set up outside. He smiled and waved a glowing horseshoe.

Beyond the forge was a large exercise ring made of pine logs. It had been swept clean of snow and held four jumps, posts with crossbars that were painted red and green. The baron and Avram, still deep in conversation leaned on the rail. Cautiously, quietly, we stepped behind a hodgepodge pile of barrels.

"The stable," Nikon mouthed. He pointed toward a whitewashed building with the same red-tile roof as the mansion. A little boy of seven or eight, in a jacket that hung to his knees, came running through one of the wide doors.

"Your Excellency," he called. "They're getting him ready. They . . ." He stumbled over his own feet, flat on his face on the straw-covered ground. He got up, brushing himself off as he bounded toward the men. "I'm to fetch Mr. Sereda." Breathless, he bowed to the baron. "No one else rides him." The little boy ran off, his jacket flapping at his sides.

We headed back between the stone walls of the storehouse and the blacksmith's, keeping out of sight along the edge of the orchard behind the stable. The snow had been swept from the back entrance and the earth strewn with fresh straw. To the right of the half-opened door hung an icon of St. George, the Dragon-killer, who, astride a black horse, had speared a flame-tongued dragon. High in the roof tiles, bits of straw marked where last summer's swallows had nested.

We stepped into the smell of horses and hay, blinded at first by the darkness of the vast space. As my eyes became accustomed to the dim light, I saw the sides of the barn were lined with stalls, most of whose occupants were invisible. The dirt floor was raked clean, the wooden nameplates on the stall doors were polished to a luster, and the walls were hung with special holiday bridles replete with bright-colored tassels.

Three men stood in front of an open stall. One, a stocky, fair-haired boy, stepped back from the group and put his fingers around his neck in a choking motion. The others laughed.

"Mitya," called Nikon.

The boy turned to us. "Hey, what are you doing here?" He pointed to a stall. "Shchastiyvliy. I'll bet that's it."

All the boys shook hands; Mitya nodded to Marusya and me. He had a squint and a grin that showed gray-spotted teeth.

"Whew!" The whistle floated admiringly from Jake's lips. "What a beauty."

Shchastiyvliy, his ears pointed up, his eyes bright, thrust his great head over the stall. His mane was brushed all to one side, lengthening the look of his neck, and his black coat shone more brilliantly than any horse I had ever seen.

"Ain't he. And is the baron gonna be mad. He's waiting outside to show him off to some guy. But, uh, Sereda's a little under the weather." He winked a squinty eye.

Shchastiyvliy neighed and pawed the ground.

"Wants to go," said a thin man with a cough who was hanging on to a rake as if it held him upright.

The other man, old with long, white whiskers, smacked his thigh and laughed, "He always wants to go."

The back door was flung open. There was a stomping of feet followed by a string of curses. The little boy in the big jacket catapulted through the door and, for the second time that afternoon, fell on his face.

Klym Sereda swayed in the doorway. "Don't like snot-nosed kids. Can walk to my own barn. My own horse."

The little boy got up and wiped his nose, then darted behind the old man.

Sereda staggered toward us, hunched over the way he had been in the strawberry patch last summer.

"Who'sh that with my horse? Whaterya doin' with m' beauty."

I slipped behind Nikon.

The foreman lurched to a stop, grabbing for the thin man's rake to steady himself. Still holding the birch handle, the slight man stepped back toward Jake. Sereda pitched forward, then caught himself.

"What is the Jew-boy doing here?" he howled. "Jew in here with my Shchastiyvliy?" He clamped a thick hand on Jake's shoulder, as he yanked the knout from his belt.

It was then that all wit and reason flew out of my head to nest with the swallows in the red roof tiles.

"Don't you hurt my brother. You murderer!"

He let go of Jake and swiveled around. His blue eyes,

the whites yellow, focused slowly; he waved his hand in front of his face as if the air were cloudy.

"You're a murderer. I saw you kill the moujik in our cornfield — with a rod. I'm going to tell the baron."

Meanness seethed in the wrinkles that fanned from the bridge of his nose.

"So. You saw." He looked me up and down in a way that made my skin crawl. "Too bad. Sure. I killed him. He wanted money. He was going to tell the baron things." He winked at Mitya. "So I take a little extra here and there. The baron's rich. He doesn't miss it."

Shchastiyvliy whinnied, tossing his head, rolling his dark eyes wildly. My eyes must look like his, I thought.

"You set our fire, too."

"Hmm. Won't deny it. Shoulda bolted the door from the outside. There'd be one less Jewish family to bother us true Russians."

"Jesus Christ!" breathed Mitya.

"Sereda!" The cry filled the barn with its authority. We jumped like horses smacked with a whip. "You thief!"

The baron and Cousin Avram advanced toward us. In their dark furs they could have been two hunting horses heading for their stalls.

Slowly, deliberately, Sereda planted his feet in the straw, shaking his head furiously, like a dog who has just gotten out of the water.

"I trusted you."

"Your Excellency." Sereda tried to bow. "I don't understand. I've cared for . . ." He looked at Shchastiyvliy, who was unconcernedly munching some stalks of hay.

124

Words began to pop from the baron's mouth. "Little extra. So rich. Won't miss it." He took off his gold spectacles and wiped them with a silk handkerchief. "He stole from *me*," he spluttered at Avram. "He's a murderer."

Like the lights in a town coming on at night, one by one, so the parts of Klym Sereda's face registered his understanding of the baron's words. "Why, I was just joking with the little girl here."

The baron, his round face red as a cooked beet, ordered Mitya to bring the carriage. Then for the first time he spoke directly to me. "Who did he kill? You're a courageous child."

Everyone started talking at once, and the horses, sensing the chaos, hung their heads over their doors and watched. Klym Sereda pulled and pulled at his missing ear, as he whimpered that in exchange for his freedom he would leave Dmitrovka forever.

"The man is the criminal type," the baron said to no one in particular. The little boy in the big jacket stuck his head from behind the old man to stare at Sereda.

Whether the foreman planned what happened next, or whether it just came out sincerely, I'll never know, but he pulled himself out of his drunken crouch, and tears began welling in his eyes. "Just one favor. For all the years. Let me say good-bye to my darling horse."

The baron stared at him for a long time, then nodded his head.

Sereda stepped into the stall, and Shchastiyvliy nuzzled his shoulder. He ran his hand along his flank with the familiarity of an old horse man. Then, before any of us

125

knew how it happened, he cut the tether and was up on his back. Horse and rider came straight for us — the thud of hooves, diving bodies, and four churning, powerful legs. We scattered, but in the commotion the thin man forgot to let go of his rake and rode it like a stick-horse halfway across the stable while the black Shchastiyvliy and his black-jacketed rider flew through the front door like a single fantastic creature.

After that everything was confused. The baron yelled orders no one could understand. Avram, solemn-faced and blinking, swung the door to the empty stall. Nikon and Jake, with Marusya at their heels, ran to the barn door and back again as if tracing the route of the escapees, while Mitya buried his head in the mane of a benign gray horse.

Then the baron gave one hard pull to his reddish beard and ordered Mitya to saddle a horse for him and anyone else who wanted to go along. Somehow, I ended up with a mule. Mitya and I were the last ones to ride out of the stable yard onto the path that led by the house. He called to me, "He's fast enough. But a sitter. Show him who's boss." The guests stared and waved as we clattered by.

We galloped under the green arch with the Tretyakov coat of arms where a wizened peasant woman stood crying "East" and pointing in the direction of the Konotop Road. We followed the hoofprints in the snow and mud, hoping they were Shchastiyvliy's. Every few minutes the baron would shout "Hang 'im."

My mule, though fast for his kind, was a mule after all, and after about ten minutes he began to fall behind.

Marusya stayed with me and yelled encouragement as I kicked and kicked. But it was no use, and at my urging she reluctantly joined the others.

A light corn snow was falling, covering the tracks. It was getting later and colder, and my breath frosted in the air. The mule had picked up his pace — I had hopes of catching sight of the others — when we came to six frozen haystacks spaced two deep along the road. Snowcapped like miniature mountains, they were twice as tall as a man, and in the middle of each was stuck a shaft of wood about five feet long. A figure in forest green appeared from behind one of the stacks. Startled, the mule sat down in the middle of the road. I put my arms around his neck and hung on, kicking and pleading into his ear. Count Dusan of Belgrade-on-the-Danube, for that's who it was, helped me slide off and without a word carried me through the deep snow to the farthest haystack where his troupe clustered, whispering, rustling like birch leaves in the wind. "*Sssh.*" "*Ouw.*" When they saw us they parted, making a path that ended at a large black horse who stood in the falling light, his mane and back frosted with snow. Shchastiyvliy. He arched his neck and whinnied, then bent to nuzzle something on the ground — a pair of valenki, long felt boots for winter like the kind Papa used to make. Klym Sereda lay on his back, his head pillowed on a rock that rose out of a small stream hidden in the snow. His beard was completely white, his face gray as the ice around him.

Count Dusan set me down. "We saw. The man from the baron's looked over his shoulder. The horse fell. Like us,

127

the man saw only what was behind him. We wander, hoping to return to a time that has passed. The past will light the way, but the future is in front of you. Look ahead. You will see it."

The troupe closed in around me, touching my dress, my hair. Count Dusan snapped his fingers, his ring flashing red as blood, and the wanderers vanished into the twilight, leaving me alone with the horse and Klym Sereda.

Later, when the baron and the others came back, we stood around the dead man and they praised me. I hadn't planned for Klym Sereda to die. That he might be hung had crossed my mind, but somehow I felt it would never happen.

Klym was a bad man who deserved to be punished. I knew that. But later when I thought about his death, I wanted to change the ending. I wanted the baron to take him to jail, but I couldn't get out of what really occurred. My part in his death gave me a heavy feeling. Over the next few days everyone made much of me, Nikon brought a box of chocolates, the baron sent flowers, heavy-headed hothouse roses, Avram gave Papa a huge bonus in my honor, but it seemed as if they were leaving something out — some words about a man's dying.

15

⬦—⬦—⬦

As the ocean, creeping gradually out at high tide loses interest in the shore and begins to feel the attraction of the big ships and wide sky, so we began to pull back from Dmitrovka. We kept more to ourselves. We concentrated on America.

Papa worked hard, often bringing home notebooks with long columns of figures that he added late into the night, and by May, with Cousin Avram's bonus and a small loan from the bank, we had enough for our passage. The day of our departure was to be Tuesday, June 2, 1904.

I still lived in Dmitrovka, yet I didn't — I was already half gone. I ran errands, I packed, I went for long walks. I couldn't help going past the ruins of our house, where I played a game of looking and not looking.

One day, inside the white wall, three black-gowned figures swayed and waved their arms. They were priests sprinkling holy water around the big brick oven, the only part of the house familiar enough with a fire to survive one. There seemed to be an endless supply of holy water in Dmitrovka; the villagers were always prepared to do battle with the devil in whatever form. Could someone have reported a sighting of Satan in our chimney? I waited till they left and went in. I looked around for evidence of the devil, though I had no idea what a devil would leave behind. But there was only the oven standing among charred floorboards and beams.

I paced off the rooms. First the kitchen, where I sniffed, then laughed. No cooking smells anymore. I stepped into the dining room and stood in front of the spot where the painting of fruit had hung. As if I were blindfolded I measured my steps to the front hall where the Serbs, their talk full of *ssh's* and *ouw's* had come in from the storm. Where were they now? Then out to the stone terrace where Sarah had performed *Daughters of the Lily Pond* for the family.

I poked around in the rubble with a stick. But there was nothing. This was not where I had lived.

I wrote the names on the white wall with the burned end of the stick. "Nessa." "Rachel." The others. The first rain would wash them off. There should have been more. When you move away from a place where you've lived your whole life, you ought to leave enough of yourself so people will know you were there.

On my walks I thought about what I was leaving — Nikon, of whom I had seen little since the fire. He was studying hard, hoping to be accepted at a university in Kiev. The one time we were alone together, he put his hands on my shoulders, kissed me, then talked for two hours straight about the hospital he would build someday in Dmitrovka. When he finished, his face was flushed, his eyes bright. He looked handsomer than ever.

And Marusya — she and I would never forget each other. The thought of leaving her behind tasted like a whole glass of vinegar.

She was fifteen now and already a head taller than her mother. She wore her dark hair in a knot, showing off her long, graceful ballerina's neck. Boys were beginning to call on her, but dancing was still her life. Her parents had agreed to send her to Kiev with Nikon to study at the Academy of Dance.

It gave me a heavy feeling to think of my friends living in a great city so far from home. But then I would be farther still — off the map of Russia. Papa had chosen Libau, in Latvia, on the Baltic Sea, as our point of departure. It was connected by railway to the Ukraine, and with a change of trains in Cernigov, we could roll west across Russia to the edge of the country, to Libau, where, my father had been told, ships left for America as often as twice a week.

One morning in town I saw Baron Tretyakov's carriage parked on the street. I wanted to thank him in person for the flowers.

There he was, walking along, his nose buried in the *Petersburg News*. At the second story window a woman wrung out a wet rag and some drops fell on the baron. He raised an umbrella and continued on.

131

"Your Excellency."

He lowered the paper and gazed at me, puzzled but smiling politely as I stammered out a thank-you for the flowers.

"Of course, my dear. Measles wasn't it?" He bent his head to within inches of mine, shading us with his umbrella. "No spots! Imagine. I'm glad to see you have recovered your health." He smiled again, bowed, and walked on.

The time had come to leave, a warm bright morning just two and a half months since Klym Sereda died in the snow. I thought how this man, a stranger really, had changed our lives. The murder and the burning of our house forced us, like gypsy fortune-tellers, to read our future, and we were warned. We would leave now, not *because* of Klym Sereda but with his help. He made us see that our government and the customs of our homeland kept us from living as we wanted.

I picked up a birch-bark basket of paper-whites that someone had left outside our door. So many gifts. Olga and her little daughter had brought four loaves of dark rye bread; Cousin Anna sent baskets of piroshki for the train, and Lev Davidov's son came by with enough mandelbrot to weight the ship down.

A passerby would have mistaken our cottage for the waiting room of a railroad depot. Boxes secured with a rope rested on steamer trunks; canvas bags leaned against each other. Every few minutes Jake stuck his head in the door and asked if it was time to leave. The three little girls teetered on the edge of wildness, tooting the bushtree flutes that Nikon had made for them.

The packing was done, the balagole ordered for noon. I sat on a trunk in the midst of our belongings and tried to imagine what it was going to be like in New London, Connecticut, at the house of my father's cousin. I had seen pictures, but when it came to walking to school, washing my hair, I couldn't get the feel of it. The sadness of leaving made it important for me to have a clear picture of my new life, but it wouldn't come.

The balagole pulled up to the house, stopping next to Sarah, who stood hanging on to her wobbly, oversized chair. "Put this in first," she said to the driver. It wasn't easy persuading her to leave it, but when we were finally installed in the wagon with all the belongings we had managed to accumulate since the fire, the Kagan family drove off to the station leaving the old slanty chair standing in the grass in front of the tiny cottage.

We passed the thatched huts, each with its separate cellar door standing a few feet away, the corn and sunflowers just sprouting in the black soil, and the wellweathered fences that marked off property lines, then into town where the moujiks called to each other across the market square and the smell of frying sausage from the streetside stands tempted me as always. Makar, the street sweeper, pushing the dust from one side of the road to the other, stopped to let us by.

Everyone was at the station to see us off. Aunt Rebecca

133

and Uncle Boris. Cousin Anna, her limp somehow more noticeable, patted and patted my arm as if to make sure I was still there. Avram talked quietly to Papa. To me he said, "I'm the baron's only banker now," then kissed me. Natalka cried and cried, her face splotched and red. Our teacher Minna Illichna presented Rachel, Nessa, and me with pink-satin bookmarks "to use in your new school." The rabbi and his wife came, as did all of our Kagan and Vorontsov cousins. The Vorontsovs said their quiet, but heartfelt good-byes, while the Kagans, pulling at their clothes, shrieked as if we were going to our graves instead of to America. The Davidovs were there and, of course, the Troyans. Mrs. Troyan hugged each of the little girls, while the oradnick pressed a wad of rubles into Papa's hand. Papa tried to return it, but the oradnick shook his head. "Books. Send me American books." Papa smiled and put the money in his wallet.

The twins, looking tall and handsome (a word my mother used for women as well as men), tried hard to smile, but their faces were as long as winter shadows.

Marusya pulled me away from the others. "Before you leave . . . I have to ask. For a while I've been jealous. I thought you liked Nikon better than me." Her high voice quavered.

Suddenly she looked like someone I didn't know.

"You don't, do you? Tell me."

I realized I might not see her again. "I'll never have a better friend than you."

The train whistle blew.

Nikon took my hand. "I'm going to give you letters. I couldn't think of a present. Once a week, I'll write." He kissed my cheek. As I climbed aboard the train, he called, "There'll be a photograph. From Kiev. In the fall."

I settled into my seat just in time to wave a final good-bye to my friends and the place where I was born.

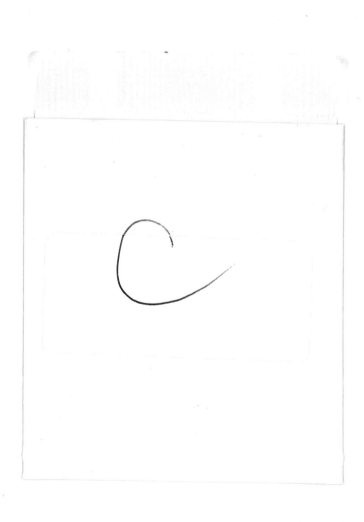